SWEET VALLEY UNIVERSITY™

D0267487

College Cruise

Written by
Laurie John

Created by
FRANCINE PASCAL

BANTAM BOOKS
NEW YORK · TORONTO · LONDON · SYDNEY · AUCKLAND

COLLEGE CRUISE
A BANTAM BOOK : 0 553 50346 4

Originally published in USA by Bantam Books

First publication in Great Britain

PRINTING HISTORY
Bantam edition published 1996

Conceived by Francine Pascal

Produced by Daniel Weiss Associates, Inc,
33 West 17th Street, New York, NY 10011

Bantam Books are published by Transworld Publishers Ltd,
61–63 Uxbridge Road, Ealing, London W5 5SA,
in Australia by Transworld Publishers (Australia) Pty Ltd,
15–25 Helles Avenue, Moorebank, NSW 2170,
and in New Zealand by Transworld Publishers (NZ) Ltd,
3 William Pickering Drive, Albany, Auckland.

Printed and bound in Great Britain by
Cox & Wyman Ltd, Reading, Berkshire.

Haunted by the past . . .

Lila lifted her arms and wrapped them around Bruce's neck, pulling his body closer to hers. She knew his kisses would make her forget everything else. Bruce's lips were hungry, and Lila slowly felt the rest of the world fade away.

Then there was a roaring sound in the sky, and a sudden and violent wind practically tore them apart.

"It's a helicopter!" Bruce shouted over the noise.

Lila stared in amazement as the helicopter made an ungainly landing a few yards away. As soon as the wheels touched the flat deck, the door to the helicopter popped open and an elegant, handsome man stepped out.

Lila's heart leaped to her throat and she began to tremble from head to toe. It was insane. It was impossible. Her eyes were playing tricks on her.

The man began striding toward her, and Lila's hands flew to her mouth. *"Tisiano!"* she screamed, before fainting into Bruce's waiting arms.

Bantam Books in the Sweet Valley University series:

To John Stewart Carmen

Chapter One

"Oh, you would *not*!" Jessica Wakefield argued with a laugh. She pushed her long, golden blond hair off her shoulder and her blue-green eyes sparkled as she pointed a finger at Danny Wyatt.

"I would too," Danny insisted, adjusting his legs so that he sat more comfortably on the floor. "If I found a briefcase full of money, I'd try to return it to the owner. It's the ethical thing to do."

"Well, sure, Danny." Denise Waters laughed. "*You* wouldn't think twice about what to do. But the rest of us aren't taking that ethics seminar. We might have to think it over for a day or two." Denise clasped her hands behind her head and leaned back until she lay in Winston Egbert's lap. "I'd have to think a long time. And pretty soon, I'd start thinking about all the expensive clothes I could buy. And the cars. And the—"

"You don't need to take an ethics seminar to know it's wrong to keep something that doesn't belong to you," Danny interrupted, a frown on his handsome African-American face.

Denise sat up, undaunted, and plucked the small blue game card from his hand. "Yeah! But according to the question here, it says there's no name or address on the briefcase." Denise waved the card in the air. "So what am I supposed to do?"

"In a case like this, I'd say the finders-keepers rule applies. Elizabeth will back me on this. Right, Liz?" Winston looked to Elizabeth Wakefield for support while reaching for one of the last two cookies on the plate between them.

Elizabeth smiled and held up her hands. "Pass!"

"You can't pass," Winston argued. "You're the hostess."

"I get to pass *because* I'm the hostess," she countered.

Elizabeth had organized the party at Danny's request. As part of his Twentieth-Century Ethics seminar, Danny's professor had suggested that class members gather their friends to play Scruples—a popular board game that posed ethical questions for discussion and debate.

Elizabeth had received the game for Christmas last year, but this was the first time she'd played it.

As a favor to Danny, Elizabeth had called Isabella Ricci, Nina Harper, Winston Egbert, Denise Waters, and last but not least, her boyfriend, Tom Watts. She'd invited them to her room for snacks, sodas, and "recreational argumentation."

The group had been at it for two hours. They sat in a circle on the floor, eating junk food and laughing, shouting, and teasing one another. Most of the cheese was gone. And all of the peanuts. Now they were working their way through a package of chocolate chip cookies.

Winston turned toward Denise. "Where do we find this briefcase full of money? And where do we find some more cookies?"

Elizabeth grabbed the cookie plate and began to climb to her feet. "I'll open another bag."

"No!" Jessica protested. "If I eat any more sugar, I'll never be able to get into my new silk pants."

"You mean *my* new silk pants," Elizabeth corrected with a grin.

"Details, details," Jessica replied breezily. "What's mine is yours. And what's yours is mine— unless it's extra pounds."

"Take it from me, neither one of you needs to worry about extra pounds; not that I'm encouraging you to eat more than your fair share of the cookies. The fewer you eat, the more there are for me." Winston waggled his eyebrows, imitating

3

Groucho Marx. "You're like poster girls for Sweet Valley University. Identical poster girls."

Elizabeth exchanged an amused look with Jessica. Winston was right—the twins did look exactly alike. Both girls were tall and slim, with long blond hair and sunny smiles. Real California girls. At least Jessica was. She loved everything that California was famous for—fun, fashion, and good-looking men.

Elizabeth, on the other hand, was a serious student. Sometimes a little too serious. It was hard for her to lighten up—which was why she thought it was nice to throw a party now and then.

"Let's get back to the briefcase full of money." Winston reached over, picked up the stack of game cards, and began to rifle through them as if he were looking for something. "Any of these cards here look like a treasure map?"

"It's just a game, silly." Denise grabbed the cards from his hand, gave them a brisk shuffle, and placed them back on the floor.

Winston scratched his head. "If there are no more cookies and there isn't any money, why are we here?"

"To examine our value systems," Danny answered with a smile. "Wow! That sounds like work."

"OK, OK," Nina Harper interjected. "Enough chitchat. Let's solve this briefcase conundrum.

Danny, how much money is in the briefcase?"

Danny laughed. "Nina! I think you're missing the point. The amount of money involved is irrelevant. If it's not yours, you should make some good-faith effort to find the owner."

"What if the briefcase is full of money that someone obtained illegally?" Jessica suggested.

"In that case, it would be OK to keep it," Nina said.

Danny shook his head. "No, it wouldn't."

Tom began to laugh. "How come?"

Danny opened his mouth to speak but was obviously stumped for an answer. His mouth opened and closed a few times, but he said nothing. Elizabeth giggled.

"I can't articulate *why not*," he finally admitted with an embarrassed grin. "Hey! Where's Maia Stillwater when I need her? She always agrees with me about stuff like this."

"Anybody hear anything about Maia?" Tom asked.

"I got a postcard today," Denise said. "She said she'll probably be home for at least another three weeks. It takes a long time to get over mono."

"There's a lot of that going around," Tom commented. "A couple of guys on the football team had to go home because of it."

"Well, if Maia were here, she'd know how to explain why I couldn't keep even illegal money,"

Danny said. "All I know is that it's wrong to keep something that doesn't belong to you."

"Let's go on to the next question," Elizabeth said, sitting back on the floor. "It's my turn to pick a card." She pulled a card from the deck and smiled. "OK, Jess, this one's right up your alley. Your best friend is wearing a dress that makes her look fat. When she asks you, 'Does this dress make me look fat?' what do you tell her?"

Denise and Isabella sat forward, leaning their elbows on their knees. Isabella tossed her long dark hair over her shoulder and gave the group a sardonic smile. "As one of Jessica's best friends, I have an interest in the answer to this question."

"Pass," Jessica said promptly.

"I'll take this one," Tom said. He began to laugh and batted his eyes at Danny. "Danny, do you think these jeans make me look fat?" he asked in a high-pitched voice.

They all groaned. Tom Watts was in absolutely superb physical condition. Tall, slim, and extremely muscular, he'd been a football star his first year in college. But in his sophomore year he had switched his focus from sports to broadcast journalism.

That was how he and Elizabeth had met. Elizabeth had been interested in journalism since she was in grammar school. When she started work with Tom at the campus television station,

WSVU, the mutual attraction had been instantaneous.

His eyes met Elizabeth's and crinkled in a warm smile that seemed to draw an intimate circle around them. Elizabeth's heart gave a pleasurable thump. Outside the perimeter of their private world, the debate raged on.

"If a friend asked me a question," Danny said, doing his best to give a serious answer to Tom's question, "I would give him an honest answer, even if the truth were painful. Because that's what I would want a friend to do for me."

"Bull!" Isabella said succinctly. "Sometimes we're all happier not knowing the truth."

"I second that," Denise said. "Let's move on. I don't think the guys can relate to this fat thing at all."

There were several murmured assents, and since it was Tom's turn next, he pulled a card from the deck.

"What's the question?" Danny asked.

"If you saw your best friend's girlfriend kissing someone else, would you tell your best friend?" Tom read aloud.

Everybody began talking at once.

"Hold it! Hold it!" Tom cried. "We'll hear arguments one at a time." He pointed to Isabella. "You start."

"I believe in minding your own business,"

Isabella said, lifting both of her finely arched eyebrows. "Period!"

"No way!" Danny cried.

"You're crazy!" Jessica yelled.

Tom looked from one to the other. "This is interesting," he said. "I sense a major conflict brewing."

"I'd tell," Jessica said. "Definitely."

"Me too," Danny agreed. "It's the ethical thing to do."

"But you shouldn't," Isabella said, shaking her head so that her hair swung gracefully over her shoulders. "When you start interfering in other people's business, you just make trouble. If a couple is having problems, they'll work them out or they won't. But whatever they're going through is between the two of them."

"So you would lie?" Danny asked.

"I didn't say *lie*," Isabella pointed out. "I said I'd mind my own business. Stay out of it. Say nothing."

"That's the same as lying."

"No, it's not," Isabella argued.

"Who thinks it's the same as lying?" Tom asked.

Elizabeth and Danny raised their hands.

"Who thinks it's not lying?"

Isabella, Denise, Jessica, and Nina all raised their hands.

8

"Who doesn't know?"

Winston slowly raised his hand. "Does this mean I'm a moral invertebrate?" he asked with a frown.

Elizabeth laughed and began gathering up the cards. "No. I think it means you're more thoughtful than the rest of us."

"Well, I guess this proves that ethics aren't black and white," Tom said, stretching his long legs out in front of him.

Danny rubbed his chin. "Hmmm. I disagree. I think when you start bending right and wrong because you think you have a good reason or it's to your advantage, that's when you start having all kinds of ethics problems." He grinned. "At least that's what my final essay is going to say. Thanks for your help, guys."

Tom put his arm around Elizabeth's shoulders and dropped a kiss on her forehead. "It's nine P.M. and this ethical guy's got at least another hour of reading to do before I turn in." He stood up and grabbed his sweater from where it hung over the back of Jessica's desk chair. "Danny. You coming?"

Danny stood. "I'll walk Isabella back to the Theta house first." He turned toward her. "If you're ready to go."

Isabella nodded and let Danny pull her to her feet.

Winston groaned. "I guess this means Denise

and I have to leave too. But I don't want to study. I'd rather sit here and debate ethical questions." He stood, stretching his arms over his head.

"Thanks for having us over," Denise said, pulling on her blue SVU sweatshirt.

Winston, Denise, Nina, Isabella, and Danny all walked out of the dorm room that Elizabeth and Jessica shared and drifted down the long hallway toward the stairs.

Elizabeth waited until the group had disappeared around the corner; then she stepped out into the hallway, where Tom waited. She closed the door behind her and leaned against it.

"Alone at last," Tom whispered, putting his arms around her. Elizabeth lifted her face to kiss him but quickly turned it away when a door down the hall flew open with a bang.

Several girls came bursting out into the hall, followed by the loud booming of a stereo.

"I guess we're not so alone after all," Tom said softly as the girls hurried down the hall toward the elevator.

Elizabeth sighed and ran her fingertips along the line of Tom's jaw.

"It seems like we're never alone," he complained in a whisper.

"I know," she whispered back.

"We need some time together."

Elizabeth sighed. She'd been giving her lack of

quality time with Tom a lot of thought. Jessica had been through a rough period, and Elizabeth had tried to include her as much as possible in her outings with Tom. Tom and Jessica argued a lot—but mostly in fun. Usually the three had a good time together. But Elizabeth missed having Tom all to herself, and she knew the feeling was mutual.

"I know we haven't had any time alone," she said, kissing him gently. "I'm going to try to arrange things so that we can be—"

Down the hall, a door slammed and Elizabeth jumped, letting out a shriek. Tom's arms tightened around her. "Hey!" he said. "It's just a door." He smoothed the top of her hair. "Still having nightmares?"

"Yes," she admitted frankly. "And I'm probably going to for a while. William White is dead. But this business about his will just seems to drag on and on. I wish he'd never left me anything at all. It's like he won't get out of my life."

"If he named you as his heir, why is his family fighting it?"

Elizabeth shook her head. "I don't know. And I really don't care. I don't want his money. His family is welcome to it."

"His family's got tons of it," Tom countered. "I think if you get the money, you should keep it. After what that guy put you through, you deserve it."

11

Elizabeth smiled a tight smile. "It just seems wrong to me."

"Why?" Tom challenged.

"It's like Danny said. It's wrong to keep something that doesn't belong to you."

"If William left it to you, it belongs to you," Tom argued. "Inheriting something is not the same thing as *finding* a briefcase full of money."

Elizabeth shrugged. "As Danny would say, *it's not ethical*."

"Let's forget about ethics for a few minutes," Tom murmured, leaning forward to kiss her.

A few moments later Elizabeth had forgotten ethics, Danny, everything she ever knew about geography, math, English Lit, and even her own name. All she remembered was how much she loved to be kissed by Tom Watts.

Chapter Two

Elizabeth stepped dreamily back inside the room and shut the door behind her. In the bathroom she could hear Jessica humming as she brushed her teeth and got ready for bed.

Elizabeth was still warm from Tom's caresses, but it was hard to stay in that romantic mood while stepping over empty bags of chips, soda cans, and plastic cups.

It was late, but Elizabeth knew she'd rather clean up now than do it in the morning. She opened the closet, found a large plastic bag, and began picking up the cups and plates.

It had been a fun evening. After everything that had happened over the past few months, it was a relief to do something as simple as having a few friends over to hang out. At least if she ever decided to write a book, she'd have more than enough material for a first novel. Her freshman year at college had been a roller coaster, a miniseries, a horror movie, and a love story all rolled into one.

She had plenty of plot. And a great cast of characters to work with—starting with her own sister. Jessica was wild, impulsive, and careened from one bad relationship to another.

It was too bad that Jessica couldn't get involved in a romance that was as healthy as Danny and Isabella's, or Denise and Winston's, Elizabeth thought. She smiled to herself. *Or mine and Tom's,* she silently added.

A photograph on the bulletin board attracted Elizabeth's attention and she stepped closer. It was a picture of herself, Jessica, Enid Rollins, Todd Wilkins, and Winston Egbert standing in front of Elizabeth's dorm. The old Sweet Valley High gang. The photo had been taken the day they'd all arrived at SVU.

Winston hadn't changed a bit. He was still the class clown—no matter how grave a situation appeared, Winston would find in it some element of humor. But the rest of the members in the group had changed completely. It was as if they had each lived a lifetime in a few short months.

Elizabeth still felt a faint flicker of unhappiness when she thought about Todd Wilkins. She took down the photograph to study it. "Poor Todd," she couldn't help muttering.

14

"Poor who?" Jessica asked, emerging from the bathroom in a flowered silk nightshirt.

"I was just thinking about Todd," Elizabeth said, replacing the picture. "Todd and you and me and Winston and Enid."

"You mean Alexandra," Jessica corrected.

Elizabeth laughed. "Right. *Alexandra*. I guess it's hard to get your old friends to start using a new name." She shook her head. "It's hard for old friends to accept changes—even though most of us have changed a lot."

Jessica sat on her bed and hugged her knees. "I feel like I've been through a lot," she said thoughtfully. "But I don't feel like I've changed. Even though I'm . . . well . . . sort of not as happy these days as I used to be. I feel a little depressed. I feel a lot depressed, if you want to know the truth."

Elizabeth's heart went out to Jessica as she watched her climb under her thick comforter.

"I guess you have a right to be," Elizabeth said gently. Jessica had had a brief but stormy marriage to a local guy named Mike McAllery. Then she'd been the victim of an attempted sexual assault by a classmate. Who wouldn't be depressed after experiences like that?

Jessica sighed. "It's terrible. Everybody has a boyfriend but me."

Elizabeth laughed. "You're right, Jess. You haven't changed at all," she teased. "That's a completely and utterly trivial reason to be depressed."

In spite of Jessica's cavalier attitude toward the past months, Elizabeth could hear the pain of loneliness in her voice. Her sister was still fragile. And she needed Elizabeth's support.

"Even Lila has a boyfriend," Jessica said glumly.

Lila Fowler had been Jessica's best friend since grammar school, and the two girls had always been fiercely competitive. Elizabeth often wondered if Jessica's marriage to Mike had been an attempt on Jessica's part to compete with Lila, who married a handsome Italian count the summer after high school graduation.

But Lila's husband had tragically died in a Jet Ski accident shortly after their marriage. Lila had returned to Sweet Valley, enrolled in classes, and tried to resume her old life.

"Before you get envious of Lila, remember, her boyfriend is Bruce Patman," Elizabeth answered wryly. "Would you want to date Bruce?"

Jessica rolled her eyes. "Not in a million years. Bruce is a big pain. But that doesn't mean he's not perfect for Lila. He's loaded—so at least she knows he's not after her for her money." Jessica gave Elizabeth a big smile. "That's more than we can say for Tom. He's got a definite fortune-hunting look about him."

"Jessica! You promised."

Jessica plopped over on her side and sighed. "I know I promised not to ask you anymore, but if you *do* get the money, what are you going to do with it?"

"The right thing," Elizabeth answered. "I hope."

"So anyway, this essay on the Scruples game will be my third paper for that class this semester." Danny ran a hand over his close-clipped haircut and sighed wearily. "Wow! This term has turned out to be a real grind."

"Then you'll be ready for a break," Isabella said softly. "And so will I."

Danny came to a stop and pulled at Isabella's hand. "A break from school? Or a break from me?" He tried to make his voice sound light and teasing, but he was dead serious. Isabella was one of the most beautiful girls on campus, and Danny had been monopolizing her time over the past few months. He couldn't help wondering how long his lucky streak was going to last.

"A break from school," she said in a reassuring tone. Then she frowned. "Unless you're ready for a break from me?"

Danny shook his head vigorously. "No!" he practically shouted. He took a deep breath. "I mean, *no*," he repeated in a more normal tone.

"Isabella, I think you're beautiful and brilliant and incredibly ethical and . . . and . . ."

"And?" she prompted.

"And I'm just scared to death that you're going to go home and meet somebody else over spring break," he blurted.

She smiled. "I couldn't meet anybody I like half as much as you."

Danny smiled back. "There are a lot of guys out there."

"There are a lot of girls, too."

"You don't have to worry about me," he assured her.

She nodded. "I know. That's part of what I like about you. You're one hundred percent honest, genuine, and loyal."

"Add insecure to that list," he said ruefully.

"Don't be silly." Isabella gave his shoulder a little shake. "You're one of the most desirable men on campus."

"I can't help feeling insecure when it comes to you. I hate it that we're going to be apart over spring break. Can I call you every day?"

"I'll be mad if you don't."

"How about twice a day?" he asked in a meek tone.

Isabella laughed, reaching up to stroke Danny's cheek.

"Seriously. I don't want to drive you away by

coming on too strong or being too clingy or too . . ."

She stemmed his monologue with a kiss. "You worry too much, Wyatt," she murmured into his ear a few moments later. Isabella drew back her head and stepped out of his embrace, dazzling him with a smile. "Come on. Walk me back to Theta House. I'm cold."

"Don't you think that briefcase-full-of-money question was weird, under the circumstances?" Winston asked, putting one cowboy-booted foot deliberately in front of the other, pretending the line of the paved walkway was a high wire.

"I think that question was unbelievably weird," Denise agreed. "But nobody else said anything, so I didn't either. I was afraid I'd hit a nerve." She followed Winston's footsteps, putting one high-top red sneaker in front of the other and holding her arms out for balance. "I still can't get over William White leaving Elizabeth all that money. Do you think she'll actually get it?"

Winston shrugged. "Stranger things have happened."

A bird swooped low, and both Winston and Denise jumped, letting out cries of alarm. Their pretend high-wire game was immediately forgotten as they clutched at each other in the near dark.

19

"It's just a bird," Winston croaked. "Nothing to be afraid of. Relax."

Denise nodded. "I don't know about you, but after that William White thing . . . I don't think I'll ever completely relax again. Ever. In my whole life."

"Ditto," Winston said, taking some deep breaths and running a nervous hand through his windblown hair. "You know when I said stranger things have happened? I take it back. I think that psychopath leaving Elizabeth his money is probably the weirdest thing that has ever happened in the history of Sweet Valley University, the history of the United States, and the whole history of the planet."

William White had been a handsome, incredibly wealthy, and well-known student at Sweet Valley University. He'd also been a criminally insane sociopath who'd developed an obsession with Elizabeth Wakefield.

He'd stalked her for weeks and tried to kill her *and* all her friends—Winston, Denise, Danny, Tom, Isabella, Noah Pearson, Alexandra Rollins, and Maia Stillwater.

They'd all gone to an SVU football game together in a minivan. William White had cut the brakes. If it hadn't been for Todd Wilkins, the guy everyone had *thought* was stalking Elizabeth, the whole group would have been killed. Everybody involved was still recovering from the shock.

William White had died in an accident involving another car. But when the dust settled, the odd twist of William's will had been revealed.

Winston tightened his hand over Denise's as they passed out of the brightly lit area of the quad onto the darker, more tree-lined path that led to their dorm, Oakley Hall.

Denise was right. It was hard to relax after being the victim of a murder attempt. Winston kept catching himself peering at every bush and shadow and . . . "Denise," he hissed, his breath catching abruptly in his chest. "Did you see that?"

"You mean the tall shadow that just slipped behind the lamppost?" she whispered back.

"That would be the one," Winston answered in a low voice.

"No," Denise whispered. "I didn't see it."

"Good." Winston sighed. "Neither did I."

Denise's fingers clutched at his arm. "Hold it. There he doesn't go again."

As they watched, a tall figure flickered out from behind the lamppost, filtered across the pavement, and melted into the shadows of the night.

"Who was that?" Denise asked. "Could you see?"

Winston shook his head. "Too dark to tell. And he made it pretty obvious he didn't want to be seen."

"Maybe he was planning to mug us and then changed his mind when he realized we knew he was there."

Winston stared at the lamppost and then looked back at Elizabeth and Jessica's dorm. "No. It looked to me more like he was just waiting there. Watching the dorm."

"Jeez!" Denise wailed. "We're really losing our minds, aren't we?"

Winston took Denise's hand and resolutely began pulling her away. "I have a good imagination and so do you. I'm taking the position that our imaginations are running away with us."

"Good," Denise responded. "I like that position."

"That's our story, and we're sticking to it," Winston said firmly.

"Got it."

"I don't see any reason to get Elizabeth or Jessica all upset and nervous just because we *didn't* see some guy walking across the campus."

"Me neither."

"I'm trying not to get totally alarmist."

"Me too."

"Good. Right. We agree one hundred percent."

"One hundred percent," Denise echoed in a hearty voice.

"Do you know karate?" he asked abruptly.

"Nope."

"Then let's get out of here." He grabbed her hand and broke into a run.

Chapter
Three

"It's getting late," Noah Pearson said, taking a last sip of coffee and closing his book. He lifted his finger, signaling the waitress that he was ready for the check.

Across the table, Alexandra Rollins closed her own book and smiled. "This was a fun idea. I've never had a reading date before. And I like this coffee shop."

Noah laughed. "It's hard to be a straight-*A* student and have a girlfriend, so I've tried to combine the two. Did you really have a good time? Or are you just humoring me?"

Alex reached into her purse and pulled out a lipstick. "I really had a good time. My grades can use a boost."

Noah watched Alex apply her bright lipstick and enjoyed seeing the vibrant red color bring her face to life. Noah was a mild-mannered psych major—not a wild man in any way, shape, or form. He was still amazed that colorful Alexandra Rollins seemed content to be with him.

Alex had started the semester as a popular party girl and sorority member. Noah had noticed her from day one. But Alex had been very much a part of the Greek system. She'd seemed totally out of his league.

It didn't surprise Noah that her grades weren't as good as they should have been. Alex had found a lot of things to do with her time during the first semester of her freshman year besides study.

When her first year at SVU had suddenly started to go downhill, Alex had made a habit of drinking way too much, way too often. But she had pulled herself out of that destructive cycle— and gotten a lot of help doing it from Noah.

In fact, the way their relationship had come about worried him. Alex had hit bottom. She'd been unhappy, confused, and lost. He'd come along at the right time and she'd reached out to him because she'd needed understanding, sympathy, and support.

But what was going to happen when Alex got her feet on the ground again? What if somebody else came along? Somebody as glamorous as Alex? Would he still have a chance?

Alex replaced her lipstick, pressed her lips

together, and then met his gaze squarely. Noah felt slightly breathless, wondering if Alex had any idea at all the kind of effect she had on him.

He was falling madly in love with her. He was losing weight. Having trouble sleeping. He even found himself unable to concentrate for long periods.

But should he tell her exactly how he felt?

He didn't want to come off as possessive. It might make her feel hemmed in. And he didn't feel like he had a right to do that to her at this stage of their relationship. She was still too fragile.

"What are you planning for spring break?" he asked, working hard to make the question sound casual and slightly disinterested. He didn't want to let on that the entire purpose of this date had been to find out what she was planning over the break.

"Oh," she said vaguely. "I'll probably go home for a few days."

Home! Alarm bells began ringing in the back of Noah's brain. Home was where Sweet Valley High was. Probably a million old high school flames were there. Guys waiting for a chance to see her again.

"What about you?" she asked with a smile.

"Well," he answered, successfully keeping his voice from breaking. "I'll probably just go home too."

*　　*　　*

Alex's heart raced as she watched Noah walk over to the cash register and pay the check.

Chicken, she admonished herself.

She'd done everything she could to work up enough courage to invite Noah to go home with her for spring break. But when push came to shove, she just didn't have the nerve.

Ever since the William White catastrophe, Noah had been a little remote. She was afraid he'd come to the conclusion that she was dangerous to know.

There were a lot of girls on the Sweet Valley University campus who would love to date Noah Pearson. And they were girls who didn't have such a troubled past. Girls who were a lot more down to earth—like he was.

Alex peeked at her reflection in the mirror again. Maybe the red lipstick was a mistake. Maybe it made her look overdone. After all, Noah didn't go for the flamboyant type.

Surreptitiously Alex pulled a paper napkin from the dispenser and vigorously wiped her lips until the vivid red color was gone.

"I can't believe it," Bruce murmured, covering Lila's face with kisses. "I can't believe it took so many years for us to realize we were made for each other. We've wasted so much time."

Lila sat up and pulled away slightly. "I

27

wouldn't say I *wasted* my time. I had a marriage, Bruce. A happy marriage."

Lila stood and walked across her elegantly decorated private dorm room. She opened her jewelry box and took out her wedding ring. "I get confused," she said quietly. "I'm in love with you. But being in love with you makes me feel like I'm cheating on Tisiano."

Bruce quickly crossed the room. He gently took the ring from Lila's fingers and placed it back in the jewelry box. *Be cool,* he told himself, trying hard not to react to the little prick of jealousy that was causing his spine to tingle. It was stupid to be jealous of a dead man. And Lila's Italian count had died only months after their wedding.

"Lila," he said softly. "I didn't mean that your marriage was a waste. All I meant was that we've known each other since grammar school. And we've never done anything but argue and fight and compete until the plane crash. Being stranded on those mountains with you . . . it was like . . . I don't know. Like really seeing Lila Fowler for the first time."

Lila's thick dark lashes fluttered and her eyes met Bruce's. "I saw you for the first time too. I mean, as something other than a conceited, rich nuisance." She laughed.

"Look who's talking!" Bruce cried, encouraged by the bantering tone in her voice. "If anybody was ever a conceited, rich nuisance—"

"If you're going to say I was *conceited* . . ." Lila began. She raised her eyebrows and crossed her arms over her chest.

"You *were* conceited," Bruce said, clasping her hands in his. "And you still are. Why shouldn't you be? You're gorgeous and you're rich."

Her comic glower disappeared and her face looked genuinely troubled. "That's it? Gorgeous and rich?"

"What's wrong with being gorgeous and rich?" Bruce asked. "I'm handsome and rich and you don't hear me complaining."

"What about what's *inside* us?" Lila asked softly.

"What about it?" Bruce snapped.

Lila frowned. "Bruce!"

Bruce put his hands on his hips. "Look, Li. I'm not going to pretend to be deep. I'm not. Sure, I'm a good student. But let's face it—I'm not Mr. Intellectual and I'm sure not Mr. Sensitivity. You're not intellectual or sensitive either. Both of us were raised to think pretty much about our-selves—which is how I know I love you. Because you're the first person in my whole life who's more important to me than I am."

"That's a pretty deep thought for a shallow guy," she teased.

Bruce's face reddened slightly. "I'm serious,

Lila. I don't spend a whole lot of time thinking about feelings and philosophy or any of that stuff. I enjoy the here and now. I'm glad I'm young. I'm glad I'm good looking. I like the things my money can buy. I love my life the way it is, but I'm not going to enjoy it without you."

Lila smiled as she walked over to her desk and ran her fingers over the litter of expensive items— the Mont Blanc pens, the mahogany and chrome desk ornaments, the crystal clock. "Being rich is funny. In a way, it makes me think more about men as people, not providers. There aren't too many things I can't buy for myself. Tisiano was even richer than I am, but it wasn't his things that attracted me. It was . . . I don't know . . . things that money can't buy." She shrugged. "Does that sound corny?"

"Yes. But tell me about it anyway."

"His accent. His sense of humor. His European manners. He was polished and sophisticated and . . ."

Bruce plastered a smile on his face, even though he felt like throwing something. Deep down, he hated Tisiano. He hated hearing about him and he hated knowing Lila had loved someone besides himself.

Tisiano had been a storybook prince. Tough competition. And in Lila's mind, Tisiano would be forever young and handsome.

Even if Bruce and Lila got married and spent the rest of their lives together, he'd still have to compete with a Tisiano who hadn't lived long enough to disappoint or disillusion her.

But he had one edge on Tisiano. Bruce was alive—a part of the here and now. Tisiano was dead.

And he was never coming back.

Nina Harper picked up the phone and pressed in Bryan Nelson's number. It rang four times before he picked it up. "Hmmm?" he answered in a distracted tone.

"You missed a fun time at Elizabeth's," Nina informed him.

There was another noncommittal "Hmmm" on the other end of the telephone.

"Everybody asked about you," she continued.

"Hmmm," Bryan repeated. Nina could hear the clicking of his computer keyboard on the other end of the phone. Obviously he was too engrossed in his work to talk.

"Well," she said casually, "I'm just calling to say good night. I'm sorry I couldn't talk you into coming with me tonight."

This time, Bryan didn't bother to say anything. All she heard was the sound of him typing.

"So good night," she said, irritation getting the better of her. She hung up the phone with a slam and stomped into the bathroom. Bryan was the most irritating boyfriend she'd ever had—and the best looking, the funniest, the smartest. . . .

Nina went over to the mirror and stared at her reflection. Sometimes Bryan went days without complimenting her. And she was a very good-looking girl. It was annoying to date somebody who probably wouldn't notice if she wore a paper bag over her head.

Nina's face was round and open, with a beautiful smile. Her skin was dark brown with a reddish glow, and she wore her long, thick hair in braids with colorful beads woven through them.

Thanks to constantly watching her diet and getting lots of exercise, her figure was perfectly proportioned. Unfortunately Nina had to work hard at keeping her weight down. So during the little free time she had, she tried to play tennis, hike, and in-line skate. And she loved to swim.

Aside from physics, the ocean was her biggest passion, and Nina felt a flicker of excitement as she thought about spring break. Her plan was to head straight for the beach and spend two solid weeks surfing, skiing, and swimming.

She pulled off her long T-shirt and leggings and examined her figure in the mirror with a critical eye. She could definitely use a little toning in a few places. But overall, she was satisfied. Her body looked firm and shapely.

"I'm a brilliant student," she said out loud, trying to practice the affirmation technique Elizabeth had taught her by directing her remarks at the small photo of Bryan she had taped to the mirror. "I'm also a great conversationalist." She flexed her muscles in the mirror. "I'm athletic. And I'm pretty."

"You, on the other hand . . ." Nina grabbed the picture from the corner of the mirror and glared at it. But as hard as she glared, she couldn't deny the melting feeling around her heart. "You, on the other hand," she said, in a much different voice, "are a total hunk, and even though you never gain a pound and can be a grump, I'm nuts about you." She stuck out her tongue at the picture. "And you should be grateful that I'm so in love with you." Nina had picked up her plastic shower kit and headed for the bathroom to wash her face and brush her teeth when the phone rang. "Hello?" she said, answering on the first ring.

"You're home," Bryan said in a surprised voice.

Nina blinked and rolled her eyes. "Yeah. I know I'm home. I just called you."

"You did? Where was I?"

"Bryan! I just called you. We talked. Or *I* talked and you said *hmmm,* and after a little while I gave up trying to talk and hung up."

"I was working on the computer," Bryan said. "You know how distracted I get. And this project is incredibly important. It's the new manifesto for the Black Student Union. Listen to this." He took a deep breath and began to read his latest indictment of campus racism.

Nina sighed and sat down. Bryan's favorite sport was composing new manifestos. His second-favorite sport was reading them to Nina. Bryan's manifestos were fiery and stirring. They were also long. Nina crossed her legs and settled in to listen. It was a good thing Bryan had such a deep, sexy voice.

Chapter Four

Jessica opened her closet the next morning and peered unhappily at the contents. "I have absolutely nothing to wear."

Elizabeth stared over her shoulder at the bulging closet. "You've got to be kidding."

"No, I'm not," Jessica said. "I don't have anything to wear to class that's nice enough for lunch with Isabella and Denise afterward. We're going to that new Pesto Café."

"What about the gray pullover and matching leggings?" Elizabeth suggested.

"They're in my dirty-clothes bag."

Elizabeth pulled on a red sweater and began to button her jeans. "How about those wide-legged navy pants and sweater Mom gave you?"

Jessica picked up her brush and began tugging it through her hair. "They're wrinkled."

Elizabeth put the soft, oversize T-shirt she used as a nightgown under her pillow. "I'm stumped."

Jessica pulled a plaid miniskirt and a denim blouse from the packed closet. "I've got to go shopping."

Elizabeth laughed. "You don't need to go shopping. You need to do your laundry."

"Shopping's more fun. How about a loan, Ms. Heir-to-the-William-White-Fortune?"

Elizabeth gave her an enigmatic smile, and Jessica bit her lip in frustration. She hated not knowing what Elizabeth was thinking. "I saw an envelope on your desk from a lawyer," Jessica said, looking at her twin expectantly.

There was no answer from Elizabeth.

"Was it about William's will?" Jessica asked.

After a long pause, Elizabeth nodded. "Yes."

"Yes?" Jessica shouted. She dropped the clothes in her hands and raced over to Elizabeth. "What did it say?" Jessica clutched Elizabeth's arm. "Are you going to get the money? Is his family going to let you have it?"

Elizabeth laughed and detached Jessica's fingers from her sleeve. "I don't know yet. So don't say anything to anybody. OK?"

Jessica stared at her sister in amazement. If she were the one who stood to inherit over a million dollars, she'd be perusing expensive catalogs, deciding what she wanted to buy. "I don't understand you," Jessica said. "You don't seem excited at all."

Elizabeth shook her head. "I'm not. It's not money that belongs to me."

"It's money that William White wanted you to have."

"William White was insane," Elizabeth reminded her. "And when you make out a will, you have to be of sound *mind* and body."

Jessica picked up her skirt from the floor and shook out the pleats. "Well, all I know is that you'd probably put the money to much better use than he would have. Leaving his fortune to you was probably the only sane thing William White ever did."

Tom smiled at the cafeteria woman who worked the breakfast shift as he placed his order. "I'll have four fried eggs, four pieces of toast, six pieces of bacon, and a glass of juice, please—extra large."

"Is that how you keep your girlish figure?" a deep voice at his elbow asked. "Keep eating that much and you *will* look fat in those jeans."

Tom glanced over at Danny. "From the way you were snoring when I left, I figured you wouldn't be up for hours."

"I don't snore," Danny protested. He turned to the cafeteria worker. "I'll have a bowl of oatmeal. Two poached eggs. Dry wheat toast. Yogurt and fruit." Danny grabbed a tray. "I can't believe I slept so long this morning. I guess it's because I was up really late. I lay awake for *hours.*"

"Worrying about your ethics essay?"

Danny gave Tom a tight smile. "No. Worrying about Isabella."

The cafeteria worker put two heaping plates of food on top of the metal counter. "What's the problem?" Tom asked, pushing his tray down the line. He reached into the cooler and pulled out a small carton of milk. "You two are getting along great."

Danny looked from side to side, making sure that no one was close enough to overhear. "I'll tell you when we sit down."

"Let's take the table by the window," Tom suggested. He took his tray and headed toward the far side of the dining room.

The breakfast crowd was beginning to pour in, and the noise level in the room rose steadily.

"You're right. We are getting along great," Danny said, unfolding his napkin in his lap. "But we're going to be apart over spring break, and you know what they say—out of sight, out of mind."

Tom shook his head. "You worry too much." He spread a thick layer of butter on his toast. "We're two of the luckiest guys in California. You've got a great relationship with Isabella and I've got a great relationship with Elizabeth. Plus, we have a great relationship with each other. The girlfriend thing is covered. The best-friend thing is covered. So why are you looking for trouble?" He took a big bite of toast, giving Danny a smug smile as he chewed.

"You know, you're right. We are a lucky couple of guys." Danny dropped his gaze and gave Tom an embarrassed grin. "I don't want to sound mushy, but you're a great friend, Watts. Somebody I can trust."

Tom shrugged. "We've seen each other through some tough times. But that's what friends are for. I trust you too." He sighed. "And there aren't a whole lot of people I can say that about."

"Thought any more about spring break?" Danny asked after a few moments. "If you don't go to Sweet Valley with Elizabeth, you're welcome to live it up with the Wyatt family."

Tom shook his head. "I don't know yet."

"Don't you kind of . . . you know . . . have the urge to go with Elizabeth so you can keep an eye on things?"

Tom laughed. "Frankly, my biggest competition right now is Jessica."

"Huh?"

"If I go home with Elizabeth, that means I go home with her *and* Jessica." He lowered his voice. "Don't misunderstand me. Jessica's great, but it's like dating the Bobbsey Twins."

"Have you told Elizabeth how you feel about it?"

"Nah. I mean, of course she's protective of Jessica. That's the kind of wonderful, caring person she is. But . . ."

Danny laughed. "But you wish Jessica would find a guy, already."

"You got it."

"Maybe she should try the personals. Get a pen pal."

Tom snapped his fingers. "That reminds me—I picked up your mail this morning." He reached into the pocket of the leather jacket that was draped over the back of his chair. He removed several envelopes and handed them to Danny.

Danny flipped through three or four of them and stopped. "Hey, here's something here from Jason Pearce. I haven't heard from him in months." He ripped open the letter, and his eyebrows shot up as he began to read. "Wow!" he said softly.

Tom looked up from the second piece of toast he was buttering. "What's up?"

"Jason's getting married."

"Wow!" Tom echoed. "That's a big step. Isn't he a little young?"

Danny nodded and smiled. "Yeah. But it doesn't surprise me that much. Jason's the kind of guy who makes a quick decision and then goes with it. Right or wrong. And as he says here, 'Life's short, why wait?'"

"Where's the wedding?"

Danny's eyes scanned down a few more lines. "He's getting married over spring break on a cruise ship—the *Homecoming Queen*."

Tom snapped his fingers again. "Elizabeth and I were talking about that yesterday. We got a mass-mail video promo for the *Homecoming Queen* at the station, and we aired it last week. It looked fantastic. It's a Caribbean cruise ship. Six days, seven nights, and it's for college kids only."

Danny nodded as he read through the letter. "Right. Leaves from Miami. Jason and his girlfriend and some of their friends are all getting cabins and . . . he wants me to be his best man!"

"All right!" Tom grinned.

"That makes me feel great," Danny said, folding the letter and putting it in his pocket.

"Look out, Caribbean! Here comes Danny Wyatt," Tom said.

Danny frowned. "Maybe someday. But not this spring break."

"You can't be serious. Are you telling me you're *not* going? How can you pass up the opportunity to see your best friend from high school tie the knot?"

Danny shook his head and unwrapped a straw for his milk carton. "It would be awesome to go, but I can't spend that kind of money. Not this year."

Tom sat back, distressed. He'd heard Danny talk about Jason since the beginning of their freshman year. The idea of Danny missing this wedding was depressing. "I'll lend you the money," Tom offered.

Danny smiled. "Thanks. But I can't let you do that."

"Why not?" Tom demanded. "I've got the money, and I don't need it right now. I don't have another tuition payment for months."

Danny shook his head. "My folks give me a pretty generous allowance, but it'll never be enough to cover a Caribbean cruise."

"So pay it back in installments. Come on, Danny. You and Jason go back a long way." Tom smiled. "It's not ethical to miss the wedding of one of your oldest friends."

"It's not ethical to borrow money you know you can't repay," Danny countered. "Look, I really appreciate the offer. But there's just no way I can pay you back. Not this month and not next month, either."

Tom sighed. If anybody could use a few days of rest, relaxation, and fun, it was Danny. The guy really needed to lighten up.

"Cheer up, Watts. You look like you're more disappointed than I am. One of my best friends has found somebody he loves enough to marry. That's enough happiness for me."

42

An attractive redhead walked by with Brent Marcel, a popular running back who looked like he had just stepped off a movie screen.

"Isn't that girl Rob Tutt's girlfriend?" Danny asked.

"According to Rob," Tom answered slowly. "At least that's what he told me in his last letter."

"Didn't you tell me he had to go home because he got mono?"

There was a long and tense silence as the two boys watched the couple pause at the door of the cafeteria and kiss.

"Yep!"

"So while Rob's at home feeling miserable, his girlfriend is making out with Brent Marcel?"

"Looks like it," Tom answered wryly.

"Out of sight, out of mind," Danny muttered.

Tom closed his eyes and let his imagination run wild for a moment. What if something happened to him, and he was out of the picture for a while? Elizabeth was a beautiful woman. It wouldn't be long before some other guy tried to sweep her off her feet. Would she be able to resist his advances?

He pictured Elizabeth standing there with Brent Marcel, lifting her lips to receive a kiss.

He opened his eyes, fixed Brent Marcel with a fierce glare, and set his milk down on the tray so hard it made the silverware rattle. "Danny?" he asked in a suddenly desperate tone. "If you saw

Elizabeth with somebody else, you'd tell me? Right?"

Danny's gaze was riveted on the couple. He nodded. "Of course. And if you saw Isabella with somebody else—you'd tell me?"

"Absolutely!" Tom promised.

They tore their eyes away from the disturbing spectacle of Rob Tutt's girlfriend kissing Brent Marcel at the indecent hour of eight A.M. and solemnly shook hands across the table.

Chapter Five

"Sit down," Professor Bing invited.

Todd Wilkins sat down in the chair across from Professor Bing's desk and nervously cleared his throat while his adviser glanced through his file. The professor made a couple of notes on the folder and then closed it. "You've had a pretty rough freshman year," he said in a neutral voice.

Todd threaded his fingers together and nodded. "Yes, sir. Actually, I'd say 'rough' is an understatement."

Professor Bing nodded and referred to the file again. "You started out well. High SATs. Basketball scholarship. Good classroom performance. Then you hit a few bumps."

A few bumps? That was one way of putting it.

Bump one had been breaking up with Elizabeth. She'd been his girlfriend practically since the sixth grade. But when they'd arrived at SVU for their freshman year, Todd had succumbed to an attack of Big-Man-on-Campusitis. He'd started acting like a jerk and pressuring Elizabeth to sleep with him. When she'd said she wasn't ready, he dropped her for Lauren Hill. But that relationship hadn't gone anywhere.

The next bump had been a recruiting scandal that got him and his friend Mark Gathers thrown off the basketball team. After that, Todd had started drinking heavily, sleeping all day, and missing classes. All of that had combined to make him a perfect target for William White, the criminally insane student who framed Todd for stalking, car theft, and murder; Todd had been expelled when the first felony charges had been filed.

Professor Bing peered at Todd over his glasses. "According to your file, you were cleared of all charges. Furthermore, it says you were responsible for saving the lives of several of your classmates. That sounds quite heroic."

Todd felt his face redden slightly. "Yeah, well . . . . We were all lucky. But I've never felt less heroic in my life."

The professor sat back in his chair and removed his glasses. "Todd, the administration has recommended that you be reinstated as a student here at SVU and that your scholarship be renewed. I'd like you to tell me honestly—do you think that you can make a success of your academic career now?"

"I don't think so, sir."

"No?"

Todd wet his lips and sighed. "I just . . ."

Professor Bing waited patiently.

"I just don't feel like I belong here."

"Why not?"

Todd shrugged. "So much has happened. I'm different. My friends are different. I don't know how to fit in as a student anymore. I'm not sure I want to be a student anymore." Todd hung his head. He'd been giving his future a lot of thought over the past few days.

So far, college had been a totally negative experience. At this point, he wouldn't be surprised if he were in the penitentiary by the time he was a junior. Maybe he just wasn't college material. "Do you feel confident that you can do the academic work?"

Todd nodded. "Sure. Academics are easy. It's the people part of college that's giving me trouble."

Professor Bing smiled. "It's the people part of life that's hard for most of us. Todd, college isn't just about Western Civilization seminars and Physics 101. It's about learning how to make a place for ourselves within the community." He leaned forward. "Give it a try. Take part in campus

47

life. Resume some of your activities. Patch up old friendships and cultivate new ones."

Todd stared at his hands. "I need to think about it."

"Are you going home over spring break?"

"I don't know yet," he answered. Todd had tried not to think about spring break. Going home meant facing a lot of old friends. Old friends who would ask a lot of questions about him and school and Elizabeth.

"Think it over," Professor Bing said. "I'm going to keep you on record. That means you're still officially a student. Continue to attend your classes. If after spring break you decide you'd prefer not to continue your education here, we'll discuss the next step."

Todd stood and wiped his sweating palms on his jeans before shaking Professor Bing's hand. "Thank you, sir. I appreciate your time." He backed awkwardly out of his adviser's office and turned abruptly, afraid that he might burst into tears if he lingered.

His footsteps rang out on the marble floor of the administration building as he neared the big, oak double doors. He pushed them open and strode outside.

Todd took a few deep breaths and felt the lump in his throat fade away. He hadn't been this emotional since yesterday, when he'd run into

Elizabeth and she'd invited him to join her and some friends for a game of Scruples.

He'd politely declined. He was too ashamed about his recent behavior to accept Elizabeth's gesture of friendship. She was moving on with her life, but he didn't seem to be able to move on with his. He wanted to, but no matter how hard he tried, he couldn't see any kind of future for himself.

Todd turned his head up toward the bright sky. If there was one positive thing about being wanted by the police, it was that it made a person appreciate *not* being wanted. Hiding out was hard work—exhausting and extremely nerve-racking. It felt good to walk across campus and not worry about who might see him.

"Hi, Todd!"

Todd lifted his hand and waved to Steve Washington, an old basketball teammate. He watched Steve stride across the campus with his basketball jacket and backpack. He looked young and carefree.

Compared to Steve, Todd felt like an old man. *I want to feel like Steve Washington again*, he thought. *I want to feel like a good guy and a hero. I want to be in control of my life.*

It was hard, he realized, to feel in control without Elizabeth in his life. She had been his anchor for a lot of years. He didn't think it was just coincidence that his life had begun to fall apart shortly after she had ceased to be a part of it.

Todd turned up the walk to the student union. His muscles were still tense from his meeting with Professor Bing. Something to eat and a glass of milk would probably help him relax.

He started up the steps of the student union and then fell back as the door opened and Tom Watts and Danny Wyatt suddenly stood shoulder to shoulder in his path.

Todd's first impulse was to back up. Tom Watts had a way of making Todd feel utterly inadequate. And Tom looked less than thrilled about being face-to-face with Elizabeth's former love.

But Danny smiled broadly and held out his hand. "Todd! Glad to see you, man." He shook Todd's hand warmly. "How're you doing?"

"OK," Todd answered warily. "How about you?"

"I'm great, considering somebody would have killed me and a whole bunch of other people if it hadn't been for you."

Todd shrugged. "Oh, it was . . ."

Danny turned to Tom. "I have this terrible feeling he's going to say, 'It was nothing.'"

Tom smiled thinly, but Todd laughed in spite of himself. That had been exactly what he was going to say.

"I don't know if I've officially thanked you,"

Tom said stiffly. "But I'd like to tell you now that I appreciate what you did to help us out."

Todd couldn't help feeling slightly over-whelmed when Tom stepped closer to shake his hand. Todd was a tall guy. But Tom was taller and quite a bit broader.

He made Todd feel even smaller than he already felt.

"But I trust Danny completely," Isabella argued. "So it's a dumb question, and I think we should quit harping on it."

"But harping on it is so much fun," Denise protested. She reached forward and took a celery stick from the dish of antipasto that sat in the middle of their table at the Pesto Café. She turned to Jessica. "If you knew Danny was two-timing Isabella or that Winston was two-timing me, would you tell us?"

Jessica reached for a breadstick. "Definitely," she said.

Isabella tossed her long hair. "I don't think any of us need to worry."

Jessica nibbled her breadstick down to the end. "I don't have anybody to trust or distrust. Maybe it's a good thing. Because if I did have somebody, I wouldn't know whether to trust him or not. I trusted Mike. In fact, I trusted him so much I married him." She picked up another breadstick and rapped herself on the forehead with it.

"Hey, come on," Denise said quietly. "This was supposed to be a fun debate. Don't get down on yourself. Mike was bad news. But when bad news comes with a great body and a cool motorcycle, there aren't too many girls who don't fall for it."

Jessica smiled at Denise and Isabella. Through thick and thin, they had been great friends. They'd stuck by her, even when she'd practically ruined her college career by marrying Mike McAllery, dropping out of classes, and turning her back on the friendship of the Thetas.

She'd managed to dissolve her marriage to Mike. But then she'd made the mistake of dating James Montgomery. After finally managing to get James out of the picture, William White had started to terrorize both her and Elizabeth.

But somebody else had entered her life, too. Somebody who seemed to be a force for good instead of evil. He was tall and dark, but he was just a shadowy, mysterious figure that seemed to step in, rescue her, and then vanish into thin air.

He'd intervened on her behalf the night James Montgomery attacked her. And he had appeared again in the Marsden garage just long enough to let her out of the storage closet in which William White had locked her. *Is he real?* she wondered. Or was he just a figment of her overactive imagination?

"Earth to Jessica," Denise said in a low voice. "Do you read me?"

"Are you going to eat that, or are you waiting for a light?" Isabella asked, pointing to the breadstick that dangled from Jessica's fingertips like a cigarette.

Jessica blinked and realized that she'd been staring off into space for some time. She laughed and put the breadstick on her plate next to the remains of her spinach ravioli. "Are we still debating the 'to tell or not to tell, that is the question' question?"

"No," Denise answered. "We've pretty much decided that you'd tell. Isabella wouldn't. And I'm not sure." She slapped the table. "There you have it, folks. Diversity of opinion and no shooting. That's what makes America great."

"So if we're finished with the great Scruples debate, what are we talking about?" Jessica asked.

"Spring break," Isabella answered.

"What about it?" Jessica asked.

"We're pretty much for it," Denise quipped. "What about you?"

"Liz and I talked about going home. I'll probably do whatever she wants to. But she won't know what she wants to do until Tom decides what he wants to do." Jessica rolled her eyes. "What about you guys?"

Denise sat back in her seat and tugged at the

neck of her pink-and-blue-striped rugby shirt. "Nina talked about getting a group together to go surfing. I might do that. But I'm sort of waiting to see what Winston wants to do. If he stays on campus, I guess I'll have to stay too."

"Why do you have to stay here if Winston stays?" Isabella asked. "Lots of couples take separate vacations."

Denise's cheeks reddened slightly. "Oh, I guess I'd just miss him. You know how it is."

Isabella smiled slowly. "You wouldn't by any chance be worried about leaving him here on his own?"

Denise's red cheeks grew crimson.

"Are you saying you don't trust . . . *Winston?*" Jessica couldn't keep the incredulous note out of her tone.

Denise lifted her head slightly, and Jessica could tell from the faint press of her lips that she had made a faux pas. *But I can't help it if it's absurd that a beautiful, sophisticated woman like Denise would go out with Winston Egbert!* she thought. And the idea that Denise would have to worry about him breaking up with her for another girl was absolutely crazy.

"I know it's hard to see people as something other than what they were in high school," Denise said in a hurt voice. "But you have to realize that I don't see Winston as the class clown of Sweet

54

Valley High. I see him as the wit extraordinaire of Sweet Valley University. There's a big difference."

If you say so, Jessica was dying to say. But she could tell from the warning spark in Isabella's eye that she'd better keep quiet.

Isabella laughed. "We should all be looking forward to spring break, but I don't get the impression that too many people are. Danny's all uptight because he's worried I'll meet somebody else. Denise is uptight because she's afraid Winston will meet somebody else. Jessica is uptight because she doesn't know what Elizabeth is going to do. And Elizabeth doesn't know what she's going to do until Tom makes a decision . . . and . . ."

"So what do you suggest?" Denise asked.

"We all need to trust each other more," Isabella announced, folding her hands in the lap of her black silk skirt. "We need to stop worrying about who's doing what and just make our plans."

"And your plans are?"

"I'm going home to see my family," Isabella said. She lifted her arms and stretched. "I'm going to sleep late every day and stay up all night reading. What about you, Jess? What'll you do with your time if you go home?"

But Jessica was staring too intently through the front window of the restaurant to reply. A tall figure stood on the sidewalk outside, looking in.

Jessica dropped her napkin and half stood to get a better look. Unfortunately the glare of the sun obscured his face.

Abruptly the figure turned, stepped into the street, and disappeared between the passing cars.

Chapter
Six

_____

Nina whistled as she jogged across campus toward Bryan's dorm. The air felt so crisp and clean, she felt like singing.

Her disposition was naturally sunny, and when she'd woken up this morning, her irritation with Bryan had disappeared. When he had called this afternoon and asked her to hurry over to his room because he had a big surprise for her, she'd eagerly agreed.

Nina picked up her pace a little, enjoying the feel of her back and leg muscles working. It was the most gorgeous day she'd seen in weeks. Nina didn't know what Bryan had in mind, but even he couldn't coop himself indoors on such a perfect day.

A little flutter moved around her shoulder blades like a butterfly. Maybe an afternoon in the sun would make Bryan a little warmer when dusk set in. She was ready for some romance. Their last three dates had been spent at political rallies and fund-raisers. For some reason she and Bryan never had a chance to be alone—they were always surrounded by his friends.

And most of Bryan's friends were kind of uptight and serious. It was as if they disapproved of having a good time and were suspicious of people who enjoyed life.

People like me, she thought wryly.

She had worked hard to fit in with Bryan's friends. She had made the effort because she wanted to be a good sport and take an interest in the things he enjoyed.

Unfortunately, Bryan didn't seem to feel the need to reciprocate. He rarely showed enthusiasm for the things Nina enjoyed doing.

Maybe that's about to change, Nina thought happily. Bryan had sounded excited on the phone. He'd said he had something to show her that was going to blow her away.

Maybe he'd put together a gourmet picnic and was planning to take her on a romantic getaway. Or maybe he'd bought a pair of Rollerblades. She had dropped hints that she really liked to in-line skate and would love a partner.

Nina ran up the walk toward Bryan's dorm, her heart beating fast. She couldn't wait to feel his arms around her. She bypassed the elevator and took the steps, hopping up them two at a time until she reached the third floor. She knocked loudly on the door. "Bryan! It's me!"

The door flew open and Bryan greeted her with a smile and a sheaf of papers in his hand. His expression was so happy that Nina couldn't help throwing her arms around him. "Hi, sexy!"

Bryan laughed and returned her hug as best he could with his hands full of papers. "Hello to you, too. What're you so happy about? Never mind; tell me later." He bent his head and kissed her deeply.

Several moments later she drew back her head. "I'm happy that you're happy," she said, giving his cheek a loud smack. She released her hold on his neck and stood back. "What's the surprise? What did you want to show me?"

Bryan thrust some of the papers he held into her hands. "These! Look."

Nina stared at the papers in confusion. "What about them?"

"The new copy machine arrived. I went to the student activities office this morning and ran the very first copies. Look at that," he said in a voice of deep satisfaction. "Look at how sharp these copies are!"

"That's it?" she said. "That's the surprise?"

"Yeah. Isn't it great?" He took the papers from her hands.

Nina felt her spirits sink a little, but she took a deep breath and forced herself to smile. "They look really nice," she said in an encouraging tone. "So now that you've got all your copies made, let's get out and enjoy some of this gorgeous day."

"Nina!" he said in a hurt voice. "Didn't you even notice what it is?"

Nina took another look. "Oh!" she said, trying hard to sound enthusiastic. "It's your new manifesto."

"That's right. Can you believe how fast everything goes now that we've got a computer and a new copy machine? I just finished writing this last night and now, thanks to the copy machine, we can start getting these out right away."

He moved toward a card table strewn with envelopes, stacks of paper, and stamps. She watched him arrange his stamps and pens and papers, looking as happy as a fourth grader in art class.

She walked over to the window and threw it open, gulping in air to calm her rising temper. A breeze came rushing in, rustling the pile of copied manifestos on Bryan's desk. "Nina!" he scolded, rushing over and closing the window with a bang. "Quit fooling around. We've got work to do. Why don't you collate and I'll stuff? Or would you rather stuff and I'll collate?"

"Bryan," she began tentatively. "Do we really have to do this now?"

"The sooner we get these out, the sooner we'll change the world."

Nina sighed. Bryan had a one-track mind. "Being a strong leader doesn't just take strength of purpose. It takes strength of body, too. Wouldn't it be nice to get out and exercise?"

"Exercise is an elitist preoccupation," Bryan said absently, beginning to fold each manifesto.

"Is in-line skating an elitist preoccupation?" she finally demanded in exasperation.

Bryan paused and blinked in confusion. "In-line skating? Who wants to go in-line skating?"

"I do!" Nina cried.

He frowned. "Why?"

"Because it's *fun*."

"Not for me," he said curtly. "I don't know how to in-line skate."

"I'll teach you." She moved toward Bryan and put her arms around his waist.

"I don't want to learn," he protested.

"Why not?"

"Because I'll look stupid," Bryan insisted. "And I hate looking stupid."

Nina rolled her eyes. Her mother had warned her against hooking up with heavy-duty political types. She'd said they were humorless.

Bryan wasn't exactly *humorless*—at least not always—but she had to admit that his idea of fun and her idea of fun tended to be different.

Nina didn't have anything against political activism. But she also enjoyed activities that were . . . well . . . *fun*. "What about a hike?" she tried. "You know how to walk, don't you?"

But Bryan wasn't listening closely enough to pick up on the sarcasm. He shook his head. "Uh-oh. Look at this page. It's off center."

Nina grabbed the page from his hand. "Bryan! I'm talking to you. We can't spend all day inside worrying about copying techniques and stuffing envelopes."

Bryan squared his shoulders and looked bewildered. "Why not?"

Now it was Nina's turn to blink and look bewildered. "Bryan!" She sighed. "Don't you care about me at all?"

"Of course!" he exclaimed. "What's that got to do with mailing out these manifestos?"

"Everything," she said. "I make an effort to do things you like to do—now you need to do the same."

Bryan turned back to his stack of manifestos with a frown. "I'm not a hiking, in-line skating, preppie college guy. I don't play tennis or work out. I don't *do lunch* or *take meetings*. I'm interested in political activism and I always have been. I'm exactly the same guy I was when you met me. Don't try to change me."

"I'm not trying to change you!" she cried.

"I'm just trying to get you to meet me halfway."

"You're trying to dominate me," he accused. "Let's not fall into that trap."

Nina ground her teeth. Only Bryan could take something simple and innocuous—such as an invitation to go in-line skating—and make her feel like a criminal.

She shook her head, listening to the little beads in her braids click together. She was going to have to do some serious thinking over spring break.

Bryan was an amazing guy. And she was head over heels in love with him. But she didn't like being ignored. And she didn't like feeling guilty just because she didn't want to spend all her time collating his manifestos. Nina was a straight-*A* student. At the beginning of the semester, her friends had practically had to drag her out of the library and the physics lab. But she'd learned to relax a little, and she wanted to enjoy being young.

She and Bryan had incredible chemistry. When they kissed, she felt electric sparks up and down her spine. But there was more to life than chemistry, and if Bryan didn't loosen up a little . . .

Nina closed her eyes and forced her mind to hold still, not wanting to finish the thought.

"Come on, Nina. We've got a lot to do." Bryan motioned her over to the card table and pointed to the stack of envelopes. "The sooner we get these out, the sooner we start changing the world," he repeated with a smile.

I don't want to change the world, Nina thought, taking a seat and reaching for the stamp pad. *I want to go in-line skating.*

"Thank you for your help, Mr. Raymond," Elizabeth said, casting her eye over the paperwork he had prepared.

The lawyer smiled benevolently. "I'm sorry this has taken so long. But wills and probate disputes are notoriously difficult to settle. Fortunately the White family elected not to drag out the proceedings. Everything is settled, Ms. Wakefield. The money is yours." He nodded toward the list. "At least, it's yours until you sign the checks you asked me to prepare—unless you've changed your mind about giving it all away."

"I haven't changed my mind," Elizabeth said, smiling with satisfaction at the list of charities that would be receiving large donations from Ms. Elizabeth Wakefield. "I wouldn't feel right about keeping money that didn't belong to me. I didn't earn it."

"Based on what I read in the paper, I'd have to disagree. After what William White put you through, I'd say you earned it a hundred times over."

"He put a lot of people through a terrible ordeal," Elizabeth said quietly. "Not just me. Lots of people," She sat up straighter, suddenly struck by an idea. "Mr. Raymond?"

"Yes?"

"Have you written out all the checks for the donations?"

"Not quite," he answered.

"I think I might like to keep a little of the money after all."

"That's fine. It's yours to dispose of as you please. How much would you like to keep?"

Elizabeth drummed her fingers on the arm of her leather chair. "I'm not sure yet. Is there a travel agency in the neighborhood?"

Bruce stared at the glossy travel posters that festooned the window of the travel agency. Posters singing the praises of Acapulco, Paris, London, Cairo, and Barcelona. All of those cities were filled with romance.

Maybe he and Lila should go somewhere together over spring break. It would be wonderful if they could take a trip and get away from it all.

But there weren't too many places in the world where neither Lila nor he hadn't been. He'd never been to Italy, but Italy was out of the question. Tisiano's ghost probably haunted every shop, every romantic archway, and every elegant restaurant.

If only he could find somewhere Lila could relax. If she could completely let go of the past and enjoy the great thing they had together in the present, maybe she could drop some of the guilt she was carrying around and concentrate on him. On them.

Bruce caught a glimpse of his reflection in the travel agency window and ran his fingers through his hair, tousling it a little so that it had some lift on the top.

Maybe Lila was right. Maybe he was conceited. Who was he kidding? OK. He was *definitely* conceited, and furthermore, he didn't think it was a character flaw. He was just a guy who saw things realistically. And it was a fact that most girls he dated quickly forgot about their former loves when he walked in and turned on the old Patman charm. Bruce was used to sweeping women completely off their feet.

But not Lila. No matter how many confidences they exchanged, no matter how much time they spent together, no matter how passionate their kisses were, she still had that strange, slightly detached quality. There was a hint of sadness that never seemed to entirely disappear, even when she was doubled over with laughter at one of his jokes.

"Bruce!"

He turned and saw Elizabeth Wakefield walking toward him, a big smile on her face.

"Thinking of taking a trip?" she asked.

Bruce rubbed a hand over his chin, scratching at the dark stubble on his face. The two-day beard was a good look for him. He hoped it made him look kind of European. "Yeah. But I can't seem to figure out where to go. What about you?"

Elizabeth stood beside him on the pavement and ran her finger along the plate-glass window, pointing to the various posters. "I'm looking for ideas." Her finger traced the Eiffel Tower and St. Basil's Cathedral. Then she paced slowly down the sidewalk, sliding her finger across Spain, Portugal, and a dog-eared advertisement for "The Balkans!"

Bruce walked along beside her, his eyes following her finger until it came to a stop in front of a bold green palm against which SIX DAYS—SEVEN NIGHTS stood out in hot pink.

"Jackpot!" Bruce said under his breath.

Jessica peered out the window. There wasn't much moonlight, and the ground below her room was thick with dark shadows. Every few moments groups of people would pass through the beam of light that fell across the sidewalk as residents of the dorms returned from dinner.

As she watched, Nina and Bryan emerged out of the dark, crossed the sidewalk, and disappeared under the front awning of Dickenson Hall.

Moments later Danny and Isabella appeared and followed Nina and Bryan into the building.

"Looks like everybody's here," Jessica said over her shoulder, addressing the group that Elizabeth had asked to assemble in her room after dinner.

Tom had arrived a few minutes ago with Noah,

Alex, Winston, and Denise. All of them, including Jessica, had received hand-lettered invitations that afternoon:

> *The pleasure of your company is requested in Dickenson Hall, Room 28, at seven p.m. tonight for dessert and coffee. Be there or be square.*

When Jessica had come back from dinner at Theta House, she discovered that Elizabeth had decorated their room with pink and green balloons.

An aqua-and-green paper tablecloth with a marine-life motif had been draped over the desk. A variety of dessert pastries from the local gourmet shop had been laid out on the tablecloth in a lavish and delectable display.

Jessica had no idea what Elizabeth was up to, but anything that involved chocolate was OK with her.

"Jessica, what do you want in your coffee?" Tom asked, taking over as bartender at the buffet.

"Just cream," Jessica answered, turning back toward the window. Then she gasped. There was *another* figure down on the sidewalk. It was a tall male with broad shoulders and dark hair. His face had been turned up toward her window. But when she looked down and pressed her face against the glass, he turned away as if he had seen her and drawn back into the shadows.

She was tempted to throw open the window and call down to him, but before she could say anything, there was a knock on the door. Elizabeth hurried to answer it and Nina, Bryan, Isabella, and Danny walked in.

"Look at the balloons!" Isabella cried. "What's the occasion?" she asked Tom.

Tom shrugged. "Beats me. All I know is that the pleasure of my company was requested this evening. So here I am."

Winston shivered and gave Denise a look of alarm. "There's something about this that's bothering me. The last time somebody went to this much trouble to get us all together, he was trying to kill us. Did anybody check the place for explosives?"

"You're in absolutely no danger," Elizabeth announced in a loud voice. "I promise. So everybody get some coffee and a pastry and then have a seat."

"I know why we're here," Nina said, pointing toward the balloons. "I bet Elizabeth has decided to run for something."

"All right!" Bryan said, lifting his fist. "We need committed people like Elizabeth Wakefield in student government. Elizabeth, I think I can safely promise you the BSU endorsement—unless one of

70

our own members runs. But even then, we'd put together a biracial multicultural caucus for ethnic diversity in contemporary—"

"The student-body elections for next year aren't until May," Winston said, interrupting Bryan's speech. He carefully balanced his coffee cup and the little paper plate on which he had piled an almond torte, a chocolate eclair, and a napoleon.

Elizabeth cleared her throat. "Excuse me," she said. "Quiet, please."

"How do you eat all that and stay so skinny?" Nina asked, sitting down next to Winston and gazing dolefully at her own fruit cup.

"Metabolism," Winston answered. "It's all metabolism."

"Excuse me," Elizabeth repeated.

"Hold this." Denise handed Winston her coffee cup and tried to find a place to sit between him and Isabella.

"Ouch!" Isabella cried when Denise stepped on her hand.

Isabella moved over a few inches to make a place for Denise. "Maybe we're going to play Scruples again."

"Please, no!" Winston shouted.

"Excuse me," Elizabeth tried again.

"You guys played Scruples?" Noah asked. "I *love* that game."

Danny leaned over Alex and Tom. "Me too. I got totally into it."

"Let's get together and play sometime," Noah suggested.

"Why didn't Elizabeth tell us she was planning to run for student-body president?" Bryan asked Tom.

Isabella slid closer to Danny so that she could lean against his broad shoulder.

Jessica smothered a laugh. She looked over at Elizabeth. "Want me to get this mob under control for you?"

Elizabeth shook her head. "Nope. I think I can handle it."

Elizabeth grinned as Jessica found a spot on the floor and squeezed herself in. Elizabeth put her fingers in her mouth and whistled shrilly.

"Hey!" Danny cried, dropping his plate in surprise.

Elizabeth cupped her hands around her mouth. "Now hear this. Now hear this. This is your captain speaking. And I have an announcement to make."

"Who do you think you are?" Winston asked. "Captain Queeg?"

"Who's Captain Queeg?" Tom asked.

Winston turned around. "How can you not know who Captain Queeg is?"

"He's in *Mutiny on the Bounty*," Danny said.

"He is *not* in *Mutiny on the Bounty*," Winston corrected in a huffy tone.

Noah pushed his wire-rimmed reading glasses up on his nose. "He's in *The Caine Mutiny*."

"Same thing," Isabella said, waving her hand in the air.

"It's not the same thing at all," Winston protested.

Denise jumped to Winston's defense. "He's right. And if you take that film course next semester, you'll learn a lot about old movies."

Elizabeth surveyed her friends with mixed emotions. Their terrible ordeal with William White had bonded them as a group. And while it was great that everybody got along so well and enjoyed each other's company, she couldn't help wishing they would shut up and listen.

"Hey!" she yelled at the top of her voice. "I guess you wonder why I called you here?"

The group fell silent.

"Well, gee, Elizabeth," Winston said finally. "We're just waiting for you to get to the point."

Elizabeth let the remark pass. If she let herself get off on some kind of tangent now, they wouldn't get anywhere. "I'm not running for anything. But there is a reason I asked you all to come."

"Is it the Victims of William White's Murder Attempt Reunion?" Denise joked.

Everybody laughed.

"Yes," Elizabeth said with a perfectly straight face. "That's exactly what it is."

The laughter abruptly came to a halt and everybody shifted uneasily.

"As you all know," Elizabeth said, "William White's will named me as his heir. I saw my lawyer today, and the White family's objections have been overruled by a judge."

"You mean, you're . . . *rich*?" Winston asked.

Elizabeth smiled. "Yes and no. I was technically rich for about fifteen minutes. Then I started signing checks. Almost all the money I inherited has gone to a variety of good causes. Causes that I hope you'll approve of. Danny, I donated a lot of money to research on spinal cord injuries—because of your brother. Tom, I made a donation in your honor to the campus grief-counseling center. Bryan, I gave to the minority scholarship fund in your name. Jessica, the shelter for abused women will add forty new beds. It'll be called the Jessica Wing."

Her friends were absolutely silent now; she had their full attention. Elizabeth cleared her throat and composed herself, naming several other foundations and charities that related in some way to difficulties experienced by her friends. Finally her gaze rested on Alex. "Donations have also been made to several drug and alcohol treatment centers," she added.

Alex dropped her eyes, and Elizabeth saw

Noah reach over and squeeze her hand. Suddenly the door opened and Todd peered into the room.

"Todd," Elizabeth said with a smile. "Come in."

He looked slightly wary and ill at ease. But Danny motioned him to come in and moved over to make a place for him.

"Sorry I'm late," Todd said, taking a seat and nodding his thanks for the cup of coffee Elizabeth handed him. "What's this all about?"

"We're all still waiting to find out," Winston answered.

"Everybody in this room was a victim of William White's," Elizabeth said in a clear voice. "He caused us a lot of pain and suffering. So I kept some of the money and put it toward something that will compensate us as a group." She reached into her drawer and pulled out a pile of brightly colored brochures. "A spring break to end all spring breaks. Six days and seven nights in the Caribbean."

She heard Jessica gasp. "You mean . . ."

Elizabeth nodded. "That's right. The late William White is going to treat us to an all-expenses-paid Caribbean cruise. I bought the tickets this afternoon. We'll fly to Miami, catch the boat, and then cruise the Caribbean on the *Homecoming Queen*."

For a brief moment silence filled the room. Then Jessica jumped up and hugged Elizabeth. "Paradise, here we come!"

Chapter
Eight

Tom sat across from Elizabeth the next morning and watched her put her glass of orange juice down suddenly and reach for the pen in her pocket. "I almost forgot. I need to call Taylor's Department Store and give them Maia's address." She made a note on a napkin and stuck it in her knapsack. "She'll miss the cruise, but maybe a shopping spree will make it up to her."

Tom smiled. "You haven't left out anybody, have you?" He gazed at her face and smiled.

"I hope not." Elizabeth smiled back. She picked up her juice glass and drained it.

Her eyes met his and turned inquisitive. "Why are you staring? Do I have something on my face?"

Tom laughed. "As a matter of fact, you do. A beautiful smile, gorgeous blue eyes, and the cutest nose I've ever seen. I can't believe how much I love you."

Elizabeth met his eyes, then looked down. "That's a pretty nice thing to say."

"You're a pretty nice girl," Tom said, smiling at the faint flush of pink around Elizabeth's cheeks and ears. "Am I embarrassing you?"

"No. I guess it's just strange to hear 'I love you' over breakfast."

"Strange or nice?"

"Wonderful," she assured him.

"It would be wonderful to hear it back," he prompted gently.

Elizabeth turned even pinker. "Tom!"

"There's nobody listening," he said. "For once," he added in a joking voice.

"OK, OK. I love you too."

Tom smiled and took a sip of his milk. "I like hearing 'I love you' over breakfast." He met her gaze squarely. "I wouldn't mind hearing that every morning."

Her eyes sparkled. Her lips curved into a gentle smile, and she hesitated before she answered. "Actually, neither would I," she said softly. "In fact, I—"

"Liz!"

Tom covered his mouth to muffle his groan when Jessica plopped herself into an extra seat and reached for the doughnut on Elizabeth's plate.

She took a huge bite, then licked her fingertips. "Swenson Travel called," she said, her mouth still full. "They said to tell you that they had to put us all on an earlier flight to Miami. You have to pick up the airline tickets yourself because their messenger didn't show up for work today."

Elizabeth frowned. "Darn. That's going to be hard. I've got classes all day."

"I'd go," Jessica said. "But I've got two classes and a Theta meeting."

"No problem," Tom said. "I've got one class and then I'm free the rest of the day. I'll go downtown and pick up the tickets. Anything else you need me to do while I'm there?"

Elizabeth shook her head, but Jessica immediately produced a notebook, tore out a page with an efficient rip, and began to write. "Sunscreen. Number fifteen. No, better make that number twenty-five. And I need an eyelash curler. Two cans of mousse. Nail polish remover. Body lotion."

Tom let out the groan he had been holding in. "Now I'm sorry I asked."

"Live and learn." Elizabeth giggled and stood. "I've got to go." She kissed him on the cheek, picked up her purse, and twirled away.

Tom put his elbow on the table and rested his cheek on his palm while Jessica continued muttering to herself as she wrote. "Cotton balls. Tweezers. Toothpaste. Rubber thongs, size seven . . ."

*　　*　　*

"What are you saying?" Nina dropped her book bag on the grass of the quad and put her hands on her hips.

Bryan and Nina had just finished breakfast, and Nina had chattered happily about the cruise while Bryan had felt more depressed by the minute. "I'd really love to go on the cruise," he began again. "But the national Black Student Union committees are meeting in Sweet Valley over spring break, and . . ." Bryan trailed off when he saw the look on Nina's face. It was an expression of disbelief, hurt, and anger.

"You're going to turn down a chance to take a Caribbean cruise—with me—so you can go to a political meeting?" she gasped.

Bryan nervously wet his lips. Sometimes he got so wrapped up in his work he didn't notice things. But Nina's dissatisfaction with their relationship was becoming increasingly obvious. And nothing could be plainer than the look on her face right now. He was on thin ice, and he had been for a while. He swallowed hard. "No," he said, clearing his throat. "Of course not. I just thought I'd, uh . . . you know . . . mention it. That's all."

Nina's face began to relax. "Well, thank you for mentioning it. But don't mention it again. OK? Not unless you want us to have a fight."

Bryan nodded and slipped his arms around

Nina's waist. "The only fights I take on are against injustice and discrimination. I never fight with beautiful girls. Especially beautiful girls who are nice enough to go out with a grind like me."

"Now, that's what I like to hear," Nina purred, lifting her lips toward his.

Bryan felt his heart melt in her embrace, and then sink down into his shoes.

"All set," Danny said, stuffing his letter to Jason into an envelope. "Now all I need now is a stamp—first class so it'll get there tomorrow."

"Coming right up," Tom replied. He stood at his desk, assembling his wallet, car keys, and jacket before going to town.

He fished around on the desk until he found an envelope and began carefully peeling a stamp from a letter he'd received. "Here. I love it when this happens. This stamp didn't get canceled, so you can use it again."

Danny frowned. "That's unethical. It's like stealing."

"It's not unethical," Tom argued. "It's ecological. We're recycling a little piece of paper and some glue."

"We're defrauding the general public out of the price of a stamp." Danny lifted one eyebrow. "I know whereof I speak. *I* took the ethics seminar."

"Have it your way." Tom laughed. He put the stamp aside and offered Danny his book of fresh stamps. "Paid for in full. I can show you the receipt if you want."

"That won't be necessary." Danny laughed too. "Thanks. Now I can mail my letter with a clear conscience." He carefully licked the stamp and placed it in the envelope's upper-right-hand corner.

Danny clapped Tom on the shoulder as he left the room and hurried toward the mail drop in the lobby. The last collection was in five minutes.

In the lobby he dropped the envelope into the brass mail bin and then rapped his knuckles on the metal, enjoying the festive clang. He couldn't believe the way things were working out. Never, in his wildest dreams, had he expected to spend his spring break on a glamorous cruise ship with Isabella and two of his best friends.

Elizabeth hadn't known that his old friend was going to be getting married onboard the *Homecoming Queen,* and when she'd found out, she'd been as thrilled as he was.

He couldn't wait to see Jason. The two of them had been friends since sixth grade, and they'd done everything together.

They'd doubled on their first dates, taking out two sisters who lived down the block from Jason. Neither Danny nor Jason had been old enough to drive, so Jason's older brother had played chauffeur. It had been slightly awkward, since the bucket seats in the front meant that Danny had to sit in the backseat with both of the girls. Danny laughed at the memory.

He walked over to the front door of the dorm, stepped outside on the porch, and enjoyed the warm sunshine and fragrant breeze. His heart began to beat faster when he spotted Isabella walking toward him from the other side of the quad. He loved watching her. Even in leggings and a long sweater, she was elegant.

"I can't wait to introduce you to Jason," he said as she walked up and gave him a soft kiss on cheek. "And I can't wait to introduce Tom and Jason."

"Think they'll hit it off?"

"*Think*? I *know*. I mean, the two guys are so alike. They're both big and dark and like football." He frowned. "You know. Now that I think about it, it's kind of weird. They even look alike." He raised his eyebrows. "Wow!"

"What?"

"They sort of dress alike, too."

"That's interesting."

"And they're both kind of intellectual. And they're both . . ."

". . . great guys?" she finished for him.

"Exactly. They're both really great guys. I think

it's going to be a lot of fun getting the two of them together. We'll swap stories. Play some cards. Do some fishing off the deck."

"Don't forget, Jason's on the boat to get married. Not hang out with the guys."

Danny felt his ears turn warm. Actually, he did keep forgetting about the wedding part. But Isabella didn't need to know that. "Isabella! Come on. Give me some credit, please. I know he's getting married. And I'm not planning on spending all my time with those guys. Because the greatest thing about this trip is that we're going to be together."

"I was wondering when you'd get around to realizing that." She smiled.

"Now I won't have to worry about you meeting somebody else. I won't be out of sight."

Isabella shook her head and laughed. "Why can't I make you realize that no matter how far out of sight you might be, you would never be out of my mind?"

"I'm looking forward to walking on a romantic deck."

"Dancing in the moonlight."

"Walks along the beach."

"Watching the sunset."

"Sharing a frozen fruit drink with two straws and lots of little parasols in it."

Danny put his arm around Isabella's shoulders. "I'm beginning to wish Jason and Tom weren't even going on the cruise. It would be nice if we were going by ourselves. That way I could concentrate on nothing but you."

"Are you Mrs. Carlton?" Tom asked a tall lady with a harried expression as she hurried past. Her big blond hairdo stuck out in all directions and she looked as if a gust of wind had blown through the travel agency and turned her head over heels a few times.

"That's me," the woman answered, looking at him warily. "What's wrong?"

Everything else about her seemed to be off balance. Her glasses sat crookedly on her nose, her blouse was half untucked, and one leg of her pants had come uncuffed.

Swenson Travel seemed to be a very busy place. All around the room, travel agents spoke animatedly into telephones and punched furiously at computer keypads. Phones rang in every corner of the room, and there was a cry of alarm in the back as one of the copy machines went berserk.

"Nothing's wrong," he answered.

She breathed a sigh of relief. "Thank goodness. Spring break is a nightmare. You can't imagine the volume of business we're doing, and the number of things that can go wrong. Right now I've got a tour group stuck somewhere in the Ukraine."

"The Ukraine's probably a really interesting place," Tom responded.

"Yes! But they're *supposed* to be in Vienna," Mrs. Carlton explained in a faint voice.

"Wow! You do have a problem. I'll try not to keep you long. I'm Tom Watts, a friend of Elizabeth Wakefield's. She asked me to come down and pick up the airline tickets to Miami. We leave the day after tomorrow."

"You mean *you're* picking up the tickets for Ms. Wakefield's group?"

"That's right."

Mrs. Carlton's face fell. "She's not coming herself?"

Tom shook his head. "No. She had classes all day, so I offered to come down for her. Is there a problem?"

Mrs. Carlton's shoulders slumped and she pushed a stray strand of hair off her forehead. "I had hoped Ms. Wakefield would come herself. She and I went over all the cabin arrangements together when she came in the other day. But we had a computer breakdown, and I've lost all the information."

"Well, maybe I could help you put it back together," Tom offered. "What do you need me to do?"

"Do you know all the people who are going?"

Tom nodded. "Yeah. We all know each other."

Mrs. Carlton's face brightened. "Oh, good. Come over here." She took his arm and led him to a computer terminal. A quick tap of a button produced a screen full of names:

DENISE WATERS	ELIZABETH WAKEFIELD
JESSICA WAKEFIELD	TOM WATTS
DANNY WYATT	NOAH PEARSON
ALEXANDRA ROLLINS	NINA HARPER
BRYAN NELSON	WINSTON EGBERT
ISABELLA RICCI	TODD WILKINS

Mrs. Carlton pushed another button, and a graphic layout of the ship popped up. She reached over, took the computer mouse, and marked off a section of the ship. "These are the available cabins. Each cabin can accommodate two people. Cabins with an asterisk are equipped with a rollaway cot and can accommodate three in a pinch. What I need you to do is assign each passenger a room number." She put her hand on Tom's shoulder and pressed down, plopping him into her seat. "Do you know how to use a mouse?"

"Oh, sure. We use computers at the station all the time."

"Wonderful. Just put the cursor over the person's name, move it to the cabin number, and click the mouse. All the information will automatically go into the file. Press this button when you're through. They'll give everyone their cabin number and key at the check-in desk onboard the ship."

"Mrs. Carlton!" a man on the other side of the room cried. "I've got the Ukrainian ambassador on the phone."

Mrs. Carlton raced across the room, carefully avoiding the tangled knots of telephone wires and computer cords that covered the floor.

Tom turned back to the computer and studied the list. It wasn't a hard puzzle to solve. Jessica and Elizabeth would share a cabin. And Denise and Isabella would definitely want to room together. Nina and Alex weren't best friends. But as far as Tom knew, they got along fine. Even if they didn't, what difference would it make? They weren't going to be spending a lot of time in their cabins anyway.

The guys were a little harder. Todd and Winston would probably be good roommates. They'd known each other since grammar school. Bryan was kind of intense, but Noah didn't ever get too ruffled about anything. He and Bryan would probably be a good pair.

And, of course, he and Danny would room together.

Or would they? A daring thought occurred to him—cruise ships were romantic. The Caribbean was romantic. With the prospect of all that romance ahead of them, maybe Elizabeth's mind had been thinking along entirely different lines.

She said she loved him. And they'd been dating for a long time now. He'd been wanting them to sleep together. But she had said she wasn't ready. He remembered their conversation that morning: *"I like hearing 'I love you' over breakfast. I wouldn't mind hearing that every morning,"* he had said.

"Actually, neither would I," she'd answered with a luminous smile and a sparkle in her eye. *"In fact, I . . ."*

She'd been on the verge of saying something else before Jessica interrupted. Maybe what she had been ready to say was that she wanted a deeper, more intimate relationship.

After all they'd been through together, maybe she had concluded that the time was right. And maybe she had made arrangements for them to be together on the cruise.

It would be the logical thing to do. What could be more perfect than the two of them, alone in a cozy cabin in the middle of the sea?

Tom did some quick rearrangements, moving Elizabeth in with him and Danny in with Noah and Bryan. Their room could accommodate three. Danny wouldn't be too happy about sleeping on the cot, but when they got there and he saw how happy Tom was, he'd cooperate.

Tom decided to say nothing to anyone about

the arrangements he was making. He didn't want to hear any complaints from Noah or Bryan about having a third roommate.

And maybe Elizabeth had broken off and said nothing because she wanted to surprise him. That was exactly the kind of thing Elizabeth would do. She tended to think things all the way through on her own before confiding her plans. This cruise was a perfect example.

His heart began to hammer as he made the last few arrangements. Should he move Jessica into a cabin with Denise? He thought about the huge shopping bag that was outside in his car. The "few last-minute items" that he'd picked up for Jessica at the pharmacy.

All those odds and ends would probably require a suitcase of their own. It was clear that Jessica wasn't going to be able to squeeze herself and her toiletries into a cabin with two other girls. Especially when one of them was Isabella. She looked like a girl who had a pretty extensive collection of toiletries herself.

He decided to leave Jessica by herself in a cabin for two. That way she'd have plenty of room for her lifetime supply of cotton balls. Tom drew the mouse across the computer pad and watched his name move up next to Elizabeth's. He smiled with anticipation.

"This is fantastic!" Jessica cried, leaning against the ship's rail. The flight to Miami had arrived on time, and there had been no traffic between the Miami airport and the dock. They'd boarded the ship by two thirty.

"Things are going unbelievably well!" Elizabeth shouted in Jessica's ear.

"Too well," Jessica responded with a grin. "I keep waiting for something to go wrong."

They had just gotten on the boat—along with hundreds of other college kids. Things were incredibly crowded and disorganized, but right now, Jessica didn't care. She felt like she was at a wild party.

"This ship is huge!" Tom said, stepping up behind them and looking over Jessica's shoulder at the pier, where kids were still pouring out of cabs and finding their way onto the boat.

"It's gorgeous." Jessica tucked a strand of blond hair behind her ear. Sleek and immaculate, the *Homecoming Queen* made an imposing sight against the green sea and blue sky.

Colorful flags flew from the ship's masts and snapped and crackled in the wind. Personnel in starched white uniforms seemed to be everywhere; they welcomed passengers, circulating on the pier and helping to sort through some of the general confusion.

There were mountains of luggage everywhere, and more kids with suitcases arrived every minute. Music blasted from loudspeakers.

The sleeves of Tom's short-sleeved Hawaiian shirt billowed and puffed in the breeze. "This is like the biggest party in the world!" He laughed happily. "Here come the others."

Danny, Isabella, Noah, and Alex were coming up the ramp; behind them were Lila, Bruce, Denise, Winston, and Todd.

"Look at those guys over there," Tom said. He pointed toward an upper deck where four well-built guys in wet suits danced to surfer rock.

With one eye Jessica kept under surveillance the pile of luggage that belonged to her and Elizabeth—mostly her.

"Look over there!" Elizabeth cried. "It's Rebecca Major. I haven't seen her since last semester. Come on," she said to Jessica and Tom. "Let's see who else is here."

Elizabeth and Tom melted into the crowd. Jessica decided to stay with the luggage. She had left this morning with three large suitcases, two hanging bags, and a makeup case.

"Where are you going to put all this stuff?" Elizabeth had demanded when the two girls had packed. "A ship's cabin is pretty small, you know."

Jessica had unpacked and repacked four times, finally concluding that every single item in her luggage was absolutely essential. After all, she needed clothes for a wide variety of activities— swimming, tennis, shuffleboard, dinner, dancing, shopping, lounging, and best of all, the wedding.

Danny had told them that Jason had extended an invitation to everybody in Danny's group. Only one small shadow of gloom clouded her bright view. It was yet another romantic event for which she wouldn't have a date.

"Excuse me, miss." A porter in a white naval uniform appeared and began loading their bags onto a dolly. Jessica looked around for Tom or Elizabeth, but they were nowhere in sight. "Can you get all this to our cabins?" she asked, eyeing the throng of people through which he would have to maneuver.

"Yes, ma'am," the porter replied. He briskly inspected each bag, making sure it was properly marked with the owner's name. He touched the brim of his cap. "Your bags will be in your cabins shortly."

"Thank you," Jessica said absently, her attention diverted for a moment by Winston Egbert as he clowned around down on the pier. Out of the corner of her eye, she saw the crowd converge around the porter. "Wait!" she shouted, struggling to follow. "Hold it!" She had seen her makeup bag fall from the top of the luggage pile, but apparently the porter hadn't.

"Let me through!" she cried, trying to push through the thick crowd and rescue her makeup case. "Please let me through. One of my bags is . . ."

The surfer music abruptly changed to a calypso tune so loud it completely drowned out the sound of her voice. A cha-cha line came thumping past, and before she could reach her bag, a pair of hands settled firmly on her hips and began to push her in the opposite direction.

"Stop! Let me out of here!" Jessica struggled to escape the line, but the crowd behind her pushed relentlessly, snaking across the deck.

Spring break was in full swing, and there was no way out.

"Bryan, come on. If we don't get on the ship, we'll miss it."

Bryan swallowed the large lump in his throat.

"Nina," he began. "I have to tell you something." It took everything he had to meet her eyes. He'd hoped this wouldn't happen. But he'd come as far as he could, and he couldn't go any farther.

He looked at the water and felt dizzy. He'd been insane to agree to come on this cruise. But he'd been afraid to tell Nina no. During the trip to the boat, he'd prayed for a miracle—like a plane crash. Anything that would keep them from reaching this point.

But now, here they were.

"Nina," he said again, catching at her sleeve as she hurried to board the boat. "I've changed my mind. I don't want to go."

Nina turned slowly toward him, and her large dark eyes grew even larger. "What?"

"I've changed my mind," he said, putting down his suitcase. "I'm not going."

Nina's mouth opened and closed a few times, but no words came out. Bryan felt like a first-class jerk.

"It's got nothing to do with you," he said quickly.

"What do you mean, it doesn't have anything to do with me? It has everything to do with me."

"Really! It's, ah, politically incorrect," he improvised desperately. "Cruise ships are elitist. We shouldn't support this kind of decadent expenditure of monetary resources."

Nina's eyes rolled upward. "I don't believe this," she said softly. "You're backing out of a seven-day cruise *with me* because it's *politically incorrect?*"

The hurt look on her face was almost more than he could stand.

"OK, fine," she said, grabbing her own bag. "You go back. I'm getting on the—"

"Nina!" He grabbed her arm. "Please understand."

"All I understand is that you don't want to be with me."

"That's not true!"

She pulled her arm away, and he felt that familiar longing in his heart. "Nina!" He ran after her and grabbed her arm again.

"Let go," she ordered.

"No!" He took a firm hold of both of her arms.

"Let go!" she shouted, a sob causing her voice to break.

Bryan tightened his grasp. "Listen to me, please." He took a couple of deep breaths. "I'm going to tell you something that nobody else knows."

Her brow furrowed and a tear trickled down her cheek.

"Oh, Nina," he whispered, wishing with all his heart that he were a braver man. He glanced around him to be sure no one he knew was within earshot. "I'm afraid of boats."

"What!"

"I'm afraid of boats. I'm afraid of the water. I . . . I can't swim." There. He'd said it. It was incredibly embarrassing. He was considered sort of a macho kind of guy—at least in terms of campus politics. He wasn't afraid of anybody or anything.

Except water.

If people found out, he'd look totally ridiculous.

"Why didn't you tell me?" Nina asked, a slow smile spreading across her face.

"Because you're this great swimmer. It's a guy thing, I guess. I was afraid you'd think less of me as a man. I was afraid everybody would think less of me. So now you understand why I can't go."

He released her arms and they flew around his neck. "You're going," she insisted softly.

"No, I'm not," he said, backing away with a determined look on his face.

Winston danced happily on the pier with a girl dressed like Carmen Miranda. She was one of the ship's theatrical troupe, and Winston was thrilled to provide audience participation.

"Cha cha *cha*," he sang happily, swaying to the beat.

While Carmen gave her hips an elaborate shake,

Winston noticed Bryan standing close by, backing away from Nina with a glum look on his face.

Bryan had looked unhappy all day, Winston realized. It was obvious he was having a hard time letting go of all his stress from school. Well, that's what class clowns like Winston were for. It was time to do what he did best—bring a smile to someone's face.

Winston began to dance toward Bryan. He'd figure out a way to get Bryan to start dancing. As soon as Bryan started moving to that Caribbean beat, he'd start to perk up. It was impossible to dance with a girl wearing fruit on her head and not smile.

"Cha cha . . ." Winston sang at the top of his lungs. He swung his dance partner around, planning to do an elaborate dip that would place her right in Bryan's arms.

But just as he lunged forward, Bryan turned slightly and the banana in Winston's partner's turban poked Bryan in the eye.

Bryan's hands flew to his eyes. "Ouch!" he cried, staggering slightly.

"Bryan! Look out!" Nina yelled.

Winston watched in horror as Bryan fell backward off the pier, seemingly in slow motion.

Winston was so horrified, he released his grip on his partner, who let out an outraged shriek. The pier shuddered slightly when her weight hit the boards.

Nina streaked past him. Suddenly she was a flash of pink linen diving gracefully into the water and slicing below the surface.

The crowd surged to the edge of the pier, and Winston had to clutch at the hands of the nearest person to keep from going over himself.

"Move aside, please. Move aside." Two white-uniformed men elbowed their way through the crowd, stepping in front of Winston. "Looks like she's got everything under control," Winston heard the taller of the two say.

Winston managed to get up on his tiptoes and peer over the shorter one's shoulder.

Nina did look like she had things under control. In no time at all, she had Bryan's chin cupped in one hand and was speaking soothingly to him while she trod water with her feet and stroked with her free hand.

Two white life preservers attached to ropes smacked the surface of the water. Nina helped Bryan grapple with one until he had a firm hold on it, then she grabbed the other one.

Winston caught a glimpse of Bryan's face as they began to hoist him up to the pier. He didn't look happy. He didn't look happy at all.

Bryan stared at the little white light and tried to ignore the doctor's minty breath as he peered into Bryan's eye socket.

As soon as he had been fished out of the water, two sailors had hustled him and Nina onto the ship. The next thing Bryan knew, he was in the infirmary—despite his insistence that he didn't want medical treatment. He wanted to get on a plane and go right back to Sweet Valley.

"You're fine," the doctor said in a rallying tone, turning off his little flashlight and rolling backward on his stainless steel stool. "You're wet. But you're fine."

Bryan sat huddled on a chair in the examining room. He was wrapped in a blanket but shivering in the air-conditioning. He'd never been so humiliated in his life. If he lived to be a hundred years old, he would never forget looking up and seeing about two million faces staring down at him while he floundered in the water like a baby sea lion holding on to his mother.

He had the horrible feeling he had even let out a little frightened whimper. *If I ever get my hands on that Winston Egbert,* he thought angrily, *I'm going to kill him. Slowly. And with lots of pain.*

"If he's all right," he heard Nina ask the doctor in a whisper, "why does he have that strange look on his face?"

Bryan slowly turned his head toward Nina and then narrowed his eyes. "This strange look is known as anger," he said through gritted teeth.

"Now, now," the doctor soothed. "Don't get excited."

Bryan turned and glared at the doctor. He was young. He was handsome. He had dark brown skin, a good haircut, and straight teeth. He was also wearing a snappy white uniform.

Bryan decided that he hated him.

He stood, holding herself erect. "I'm leaving," he announced, throwing the blanket around him with as much dignity as he could muster. He moved slowly toward the door, holding his head high and taking long, measured strides.

"Where are you going?" Nina wailed.

"I'm going home."

"I'm afraid you can't leave," the doctor said.

"Oh?" Bryan asked, lifting one eyebrow. "And why not?"

"The ship has already sailed." The doctor gave Nina a conspiratorial wink and then began to laugh. He had a deep, booming masculine laugh. Nina joined in, giggling. Bryan scowled.

"That was a truly impressive rescue," the doctor said, focusing his full attention on Nina. "You're a very brave woman."

"Oh, no," she said modestly.

"You must have studied swimming for many years."

"I did. Up until college."

"Really," the doctor said. "Me too. I wanted to

try out for the Olympics, but my parents were afraid it would take too much time away from my schoolwork."

Nina nodded seriously, as if she'd never heard anything more interesting. "That would be a really difficult decision."

"I grew up in upstate New York," the doctor said. "What about you?"

Bryan couldn't believe it. The guy was actually trying to make a move on Nina. The jerk thought he could charm her right in front of Bryan's eyes. Wasn't that against the Hippocratic oath or something?

Nina was giggling again, and the doctor's phony chuckle was getting on Bryan's nerves. It was time to break up the party.

"Excuse me," he said, clearing his throat.

Both of them broke off and looked at him as if they had forgotten he was there.

"I have a headache," Bryan informed them. "Would it be possible for you to get me an aspirin, Doctor . . . ?" He trailed off and lifted an interrogative eyebrow.

"Dr. Daniels," the doctor said helpfully, turning to his medicine cabinet.

Nina stood at the doctor's elbow. "Oh, look! Tea Tree oil. I love the way that smells. What do you use it for, Dr. Daniels?"

"My name is Richard," he said to Nina. He

smiled broadly, showing both rows of white, evenly spaced teeth. "My friends call me Rich."

Nina smiled and Bryan ground his teeth. *Rich!* Just the kind of pseudo-macho name he'd expect from a low-down, girl-stealing, mint-sucking, preppie cruise quack.

Chapter
Ten

"Wow!" Denise whistled. "This is unbelievable. I can see the water through our porthole."

Isabella hung up a long black dress with cap sleeves and a low back. It was made of a jersey with a nice heavy drape and had traveled beautifully. No wrinkles at all.

She couldn't wait to dance with Danny in the moonlight with the hem moving gracefully around her ankles.

"Poor Bryan," Denise said, happily inspecting their cabin. She was putting away her things and trying to change clothes at the same time. "I can't believe what happened. Winston feels really bad about it."

"I'm sure Bryan's not angry," Isabella said.

"He sure looked angry." Denise sat down on her bed and bounced a little. "I hope it wasn't a sign of an inauspicious start. You know, a lot of things can go wrong on a cruise. Look what happened on the *Titanic*."

"Don't be silly," Isabella said. "Everybody's going to have a great time. And I don't think there are any icebergs in the Caribbean."

"I don't know about that," Denise said slowly. "I tried to talk to Danny on the pier, but he really gave me the cold shoulder. Is he mad at me or something?"

Isabella laughed. "He was just mad because the cabdriver overcharged us for the ride. It offended his sense of ethics. But he was happy by the time we got on the ship. There was a message for him when we boarded. It said to meet Jason and his fiancée on the café deck when we got settled."

"And I'm supposed to meet Winston as soon as I get changed." Denise peeled off her T-shirt and shorts and reached down into her duffel bag. "Ta-da! Look at this." She held up a bright forties-style sundress.

"That's great," Isabella commented as Denise pulled it on.

"And that's not all," Denise said. She reached into her bag and produced a pair of beach shoes with seashells glued to the toes. "Aren't they tacky?"

"Totally tacky," Isabella agreed.

Denise laughed. "If you think these are bad,

wait till you see Winston's Bermuda shorts. Green and purple."

There was a knock on the door and Denise opened it.

"Wow! This is nice," Danny said, stepping into the cabin. "Bigger than mine. Somehow I got put in with Noah and Bryan." He put a hand on Denise's shoulder and squeezed. "I'm sorry if I was a grump on the pier. I wasn't mad at you."

"There are three of you in a cabin?" Isabella frowned. "How could they make a mistake like that?"

Danny shrugged. "You know how these things are. Sometimes travel agents get the arrangements mixed up."

"Do you think Bryan is capable of violence?" Winston asked Todd as the two boys unpacked their bags. Winston threw a couple of pairs of socks into a drawer.

Todd smiled. "I guess everybody is capable of violence under certain circumstances. But if you're asking me, do I think Bryan will punch you in the nose when he sees you, the answer is no."

"Because deep down he knows that problem solving through violence is no solution and that in spite of our unfortunate contretemps, I had only his best interests at heart?"

"No," Todd answered simply. "Because Nina won't let him."

"Oh!" Winston's face fell.

Todd laughed. He was glad he and Winston were rooming together. It was like being back in high school on some kind of class trip. The sordid events of the past few months seemed more remote now. Standing here, laughing at Winston's antics, made him feel like the old Todd Wilkins. Todd the high school hero.

Todd reached into the closet and found some hangers. There was a knock on the door and Denise walked in. "Ready to go swank around the deck in our drop-dead cruise wear?" she asked, stepping inside the cabin and smiling at Todd.

"Great outfit," he said.

"What do you think of this?" Winston asked, pulling a shirt from his suitcase and holding it up against him.

Todd made a gagging sound. He'd never seen such a horrible shirt in his whole life. It was a hideous acid green with big black and purple palm trees on it.

Winston slipped it on, buttoned it up, and did a little strut around the cabin.

"That's the weirdest shirt I've ever seen," Todd said.

Winston's face brightened. "Thanks!"

Denise took his arm and handed Todd a camera. "Will you take our picture?"

"Sure." Todd stepped back and lifted the camera to focus. He watched through the lens as Denise stood on her tiptoes and put her cheek next to Winston's. Both of them smiled, and Todd pressed the zoom, going for a close-up of their happy faces.

They looked perfectly matched and totally in love. Just like he and Elizabeth had looked less than a year ago.

The picture went blurry. Todd reached around to adjust the lens but stopped when he realized it wasn't the lens that was making the picture fuzzy.

Horrified, he wiped away a tear that was rolling down his cheek. He snapped the picture and turned away, rubbing his eyes with his sleeves.

"Something in your eye?" Winston asked.

Todd nodded, unable to trust his voice to speak.

"We're going to poke around and see what's where," Denise said. "Want to come with us?"

Todd cleared his throat. "No, thanks," he said. "I'll just . . ." He trailed off, stumped. *Just what?* He had no one to meet and no place to be. "I've got some things to do," he said vaguely. "I'll see you guys around."

Denise and Winston left, teasing each other as they walked out the door.

Alone, Todd sighed, staring out the porthole at the vast, empty ocean.

* * *

Elizabeth examined the key she had picked up at the check-in desk. Cabin number 442. Getting checked in had taken forever. She'd seen lots of people from SVU and even some familiar faces from high school. There were students from colleges all over the country, and some of the big universities had set up hospitality booths on the main deck.

The booth staff had been eager to extend hospitality to virtually everybody who went by. Elizabeth had drunk at least a half-dozen Cokes and met a hundred people in the past hour.

But now she was ready to get settled. She followed the signs and descended a set of stairs to a lower deck. Then she paused at a corner and examined a small map. It looked as if her cabin should be nearby. "Aha!" she said out loud when she encountered the number 442 elegantly etched on a brass plate mounted on the cabin door. She turned the key in the door and stepped into the cabin.

As promised, her bags were waiting for her. They sat on the luggage rack. A large bottle of sparkling water was open on the bureau, and one of the paper-wrapped glasses sat on the tray half full.

The bathroom door was closed, but she could hear water running inside. "Jessica!"

She heard the water turn off.

"Jess, it's me. Have you ever seen anything like this place in your life?"

"No," answered a deep baritone. "I never have."

The door opened and Elizabeth's eyes widened.

Chapter
Eleven

Tom knew immediately that he had miscalculated. He could tell by the expression on Elizabeth's face. She looked embarrassed and irritated—and her cheeks were flushed red.

"I take it this isn't what you had in mind?" he said, feeling pretty embarrassed and irritated himself. "I'm sorry. I don't mean to push, but I really thought you were ready. I thought that this was what you wanted."

Elizabeth put down her purse. "How did you set this up?" she asked.

"At the travel agency. They lost all the information you gave them about accommodations and asked me if I knew who was rooming with who."

"And you thought I wanted us to room together?"

Tom paused, then nodded.

"Tom," she began. "If I'd made a decision to sleep with you, I'd tell you. We'd discuss it together. It's not the kind of thing I'd surprise you with. I'm sorry if I gave you the wrong signals, but . . ."

Tom held up his hand and cut her off. "Don't be sorry." He reached for his jacket and his suitcase. "I'll move down to Jessica's cabin, bring her stuff here, and tell Danny to move in with me." He let out rueful laugh. "Jessica won't be too happy about it, but I'm sure Danny will be thrilled. I crammed him in with Bryan and Noah."

"Are you disappointed?" she asked softly.

"Of course," he answered, sounding more curt than he meant to. As he walked down the hall, he realized that more than anything else, he felt mortified. He'd taken a chance, guessed wrong, and the result was that he had given Elizabeth a chance to shoot him down yet again.

I'd tell you. We'd discuss it together.

How was he supposed to know that? The truth was, she hadn't been telling him much of anything recently.

She'd been very secretive about her dealings with William White and the lawyer. And she hadn't consulted anybody else about this cruise thing. She'd just made a unilateral decision that they were all going on a cruise, and now here they were.

Tom wasn't unhappy about being here. Far from it. But it was the principle of the matter. Elizabeth seemed to take it for granted that she was going to do all the thinking—and then inform him of her decision. It was like he didn't have any rights at all.

By the time Tom reached the cabin he would be occupying with Danny, he heard Danny's voice calling him. "Tom! Wait up!"

Tom turned and saw Danny hurrying toward him. "There's been a mistake," Tom said. "You and I are in this cabin together." He gestured toward the door with his head.

"All right!" Danny said happily. "I'll move my stuff in a little while. Listen, I just saw Jason and his fiancée. Wow! Is she gorgeous! What are you and Elizabeth doing for dinner?"

"I don't know," Tom answered in a sour tone. "She hasn't informed me yet."

But Danny seemed too excited to notice the unhappy catch in Tom's voice. "Plan on sitting with me, Isabella, and Jason and his girlfriend. I really want you guys to meet."

"When and where?"

"The main dining room. Eight o'clock."

"We'll be there," Tom said. *Unless Elizabeth has a problem with that*, he added mentally as Danny hurried away.

* * *

"If that was a *snack* . . ." Winston said in a voice of disbelief, "I can't wait to see what they call dinner." He put his hand over his full stomach and groaned. "Where I come from, an afternoon snack is a couple of graham crackers and a glass of milk."

Denise didn't even bother to answer. She flopped into a deck chair and groaned.

They had just left the café deck, where afternoon tea had been served. A long buffet table, lined with platters, was covered with a snowy white cloth.

Winston had never seen so much food in his life. There had been a dozen different kinds of sandwiches. Avocado halves stuffed with crabmeat and drizzled with olive oil. Baskets of rolls. Mountains of strawberries. Platters of melon and pineapple. And it had all looked delicious.

Winston and Denise had fallen on the buffet and worked their way from one end to the other, determined to taste everything.

"I don't think I'll eat again for the rest of the cruise," Winston said with a sigh.

Denise took a deep breath. "You'll change your mind. This sea air gives you an appetite."

Winston watched the steady stream of passengers strolling around the deck. It was late in the afternoon, and people were beginning to wander out and explore the ship after settling into their cabins.

The ship was truly an amazing thing, Winston reflected. It was unbelievable that modern technology could fuse a fancy hotel with two dining rooms, a pool, a gym, a bowling alley, two theaters, four gift and clothing shops, a shuffleboard deck, a skeet-shooting range, a disco, a hair salon, and a dozen other places to meet, greet, and eat. And that it could all float!

"Here come Bryan and Nina," Denise said under her breath. "Should we make ourselves scarce?"

Winston peered over his sunglasses and studied Bryan's face. He didn't look violent. But he didn't look happy. He had that same glum, down-in-the-dumps expression on his face that he had worn ever since they left SVU.

"Nope!" Winston said, coming to a decision. "I'm not going to avoid him. It was my fault he went over the side. It's my responsibility to make it up to him. Come on." He pulled himself out of the deck chair.

Denise jumped to her feet and caught at his sleeve. "Maybe we should just let him and Nina walk around on their own. Maybe they're not in the mood for company."

"People do not come on cruises to hang out by themselves," Winston said sagely. "Oh, sure. They may put on a grumpy face and give off keep-away vibes. But it's a defense. A protective armor to disguise emotional vulnerability."

"Where are you getting this stuff?"

"From Noah," Winston explained. "Our resident amateur psychologist. We had a long talk on the airplane while you were asleep."

"About Bryan?"

Winston frowned. "No. About me. But hey! Class clown. Cruise curmudgeon. What's the difference?" He put his arm around Denise and pulled her close. "You see, the reason Bryan is afraid to get close to me is that he's afraid of being hurt."

"I think Bryan is afraid you'll push him over the side again," Denise said flatly.

"Watch that word *push*, OK?" Winston said. "I didn't *push* him. *Bumped*? Yes. *Jostled*? Perhaps. But *push*?" Winston drew himself up. "Never!"

Denise giggled. "Well, whatever you call it, I think he's afraid you'll do it to him again."

Winston took her hand. "Come on. Let's see if we can't make peace. Yo, Bryan!" he called.

When Bryan turned, the unfriendly glint in his eye was so intense that it took all of Winston's self-control not to back up and run. Instead, he resolutely plowed forward. "I know I've said it already, but I'm really sorry about what happened on the pier." Winston held out his hand to Bryan. "Can we shake and be friends again?"

For a moment, Winston thought Bryan was actually going to refuse. But Nina elbowed him in the arm, and after a few tense seconds Bryan took Winston's hand. Almost immediately Bryan's face began to relax.

It was amazing what a determined overture of friendship could accomplish, Winston noted. There was a lesson in diplomacy to be learned here. Bryan had been determined to hate him. But Winston had overborne his antipathy by sheer force of goodwill. He'd disarmed him with a sincere desire to be friends.

Winston pictured himself shaking hands with some foreign dignitary, having just concluded a world-disarmament pact. Global peace was closer than they had all dreamed. It was just a whoopee cushion and a banana peel away.

"Winston!" Denise said sharply.

Winston blinked, realizing that the conversation had moved on while he'd been daydreaming—and he was still pumping Bryan's hand. Embarrassed, he let go and noticed that Bryan flexed his fingers, making sure nothing was damaged. "Uh, sorry. I guess I spaced out for a minute."

"We've been trying to decide what to do," Nina explained.

"How about some tennis?" Denise suggested.

Bryan shook his head. "I don't know how to play tennis."

Denise chewed a cuticle. "There's a putting green on the upper deck."

"I don't know how to play golf, either," Bryan answered.

"Skeet shooting?" Winston ventured.

"Guns are too dangerous," Bryan responded.

"How about shuffleboard?" Winston suggested. "It's safe. Really safe. And it's the national sport of Miami."

The group laughed and climbed the metal stairs that led to the next deck. There were shuffleboard lines painted all over its floor. Winston and Denise took charge and quickly located poles and pucks.

"OK, now!" Winston said. "Does everybody know how to play?"

"I've never actually played," Nina said, giving her puck an experimental push. "But I've seen my grandparents play it at their country club."

Winston wasn't sure, but he thought he saw Bryan grimace. "My grandparents didn't belong to a country club," Bryan said in a flat voice. "So I guess you'll have to show me what I'm supposed to do."

Nina rolled her eyes. "Don't turn this into a big class war, OK? It's just shuffleboard."

Winston jumped in, determined to pour Egbert's oil on the troubled waters. "Bryan, shuffleboard is a game for everybody," he said expansively. "All you have to do is take this long pole and place it against the puck, like so. . . ." He carefully positioned the pole so that it rested against the solid black disk. "Then you give it a hard shove—like this." Winston leaned forward, putting all his weight behind the pole. "And you push."

The deck was slick, and Winston wound up putting a little more spin on the shove than he'd intended to. The puck went airborne, and as it hurtled through the air it clipped Bryan above his left eye, knocking him backward.

"Ouch!" Bryan yelled, hitting the ground and banging the back of his head on the solid steel deck.

Horrified, Winston ran over to where Bryan lay flat on his back. Blood flowed from a gash above his eye. He shot an accusing glare up at Winston just before his thick lashes fluttered shut.

Chapter
Twelve

Todd pushed the food around on his plate with his fork and tried to look happy about sitting at the huge round table by himself. He'd arrived at the café deck for afternoon tea just as Denise and Winston had come rolling out.

All around him there were groups of college kids sitting at the large tables.

Todd looked down at his full plate. He'd thought he was hungry after he'd showered and changed clothes. But now his appetite was gone, and there was a large knot in the pit of his stomach.

Behind him a table full of pretty girls wearing matching University of Virginia sweatshirts burst into laughter. To his left, a group of jocks from Alaska teased each other about dropped balls and missed baskets.

There was a time when Todd could have walked over to those guys and simply introduced himself. Just a few months ago, he would have felt comfortable joining any group in the room. Now he couldn't imagine walking up to a group of strangers and trying to strike up a conversation.

Give it a try, Professor Bing had said. *Take part in campus life. Resume some of your activities. Patch up old friendships and cultivate new ones.*

Todd took a deep breath. Maybe his adviser was right. Todd had been feeling sorry for himself long enough—he needed to make a concerted effort to get his old life back. Three girls, including a tall blonde, sat by themselves at the next table. He'd pick up his plate, walk over, and ask if he could join them.

Todd's fingers gripped the edge of the white china plate and he half stood just as the tall blonde turned in her seat to look at the room. Her eyes looked right through him, then flickered past him without a pause. He'd never seen anybody look so completely disinterested.

He sat back down, abandoning his plan to join her. *I wish I'd stayed in Sweet Valley,* he thought miserably. Todd dropped his fork and sat back, staring at the starched aprons on the smiling chefs who were serving food. Finally he put his napkin on the table and stood. "I've got to get out of here," he muttered to himself.

As he made his way through the dining room, he felt incredibly conspicuous. Conspicuously alone. How was he going to survive a week of this?

Todd forced a smile and politely excused himself as he tried to ease his way through a cluster of giggling girls who blocked the door to the deck. Suddenly his foot came down on something soft, and he heard a high-pitched cry. He looked around the group of female faces to see who he had stepped on. His eyes rested on a lovely Asian face twisted in pain. He took her arm so that she wouldn't stumble. "I'm so sorry," he said. "Are you all right?"

"Don't apologize," she said, giving him a tight smile. "That's what I get for standing in the doorway."

He helped her hop away from the door and watched as she removed her loafer and massaged her toe. "Is anything broken?" he asked anxiously.

She shook her head. "Nah. But you're sweet to be so worried." She smiled again. "You're Todd Wilkins."

He nodded. "That's right. And you look familiar. Sweet Valley University, right?"

"Right. We were in a class together last semester. World History. Section I."

"That section met in the Stadium. How could you remember anybody from that class?"

They both laughed. World History was one of the largest freshman sections offered at SVU. It took place in a huge auditorium the students jokingly called the Stadium, since it seated so many people.

"Well, mostly I know who you are because I'm a big basketball fan," she said.

"Oh," Todd said, feeling his heart sink. If she was a basketball fan, that meant she probably knew about the recruiting scandal. But like everybody else, she wouldn't have followed it closely enough to realize that he'd never actually done anything wrong. He'd just been a scapegoat.

"You really got a raw deal," she said.

His brows lifted in surprise. "You think so?"

"I know so. I was pretty obsessed with that story last semester."

"You must be very interested in sports."

She shrugged. "I'm into sportswriting. I was the head sportswriter for my high school paper. And I write a column for the SVU newspaper."

Todd nodded. "Now I know who you are. You're Gin-Yung Suh. I've read a lot of your stuff. But I thought you were a guy."

"Everybody does. Nobody ever sees a sports byline and figures that the writer is a woman."

"Gin-Yung," Todd repeated. "Chinese?"

"Korean. My granddad learned English when he was a young man by reading out loud from the sports pages. He fell in love with Red Smith and Grantland Rice. Those were the big sportswriters in his day. They're, like, classicists. Anyway, he saved their columns and read their stuff to me when I was growing up. It was more exciting than fairy tales." She laughed. "Those guys were my Hans Christian Andersen and Mother Goose. The upshot is that I'd decided to be a sportswriter by the time I was eight years old."

She slipped her loafer back on and gave him an interested smile. "I follow high school and college sports all over the country. So I'd heard of you and Mark Gathers before I ever got to the SVU campus." She grinned. "Boy, was I thrilled when I saw the varsity lineup. Gathers and Wilkins. Wow!" She began walking, slowly letting her stride return to normal.

"Sorry we let you down," Todd said wryly, falling into step beside her.

She shrugged and waved her hand. "That's sports! Win some, lose some. I had a feeling Mark Gathers was getting paid—flashy car, expensive clothes. It wasn't the typical freshman lifestyle. You, though? I never understood how you got sandbagged."

"It's a long story," he said softly. "But I may be back on the team next year. They've given me the option. I'll have to think about it."

"What's to think about?"

He pulled at the neck of his shirt. "That's kind of a broad question." They went over to the rail and looked out at the sea. "It's been . . ."

"A strange year?" she said, leaning over the rail. "No kidding. That William White story was like something out of the movies. And what you did was truly heroic."

"You seem to know a lot about me."

"Only what I read in the papers. As I recall, the newspaper called your plan 'a brilliant stroke.'"

Todd shook his head. "Brilliant? I don't think so. Try desperate. I had no idea whether or not it would work. All I knew was that I had to try something. I'm just thankful that everyone was OK."

Tom, Danny, Isabella, Denise, Winston, Maia Stillwater, Bryan, Nina, and Jessica had all been trapped in a van racing along a curvy mountain road with the brakes cut. With every passing mile the van picked up speed, taking the turns faster and faster.

Todd had remembered a steep, uphill private road and had led the van up the road until it lost momentum and the passengers were able to jump out and roll to safety.

"Have you always been this modest?" she asked in a teasing tone.

"No!" Todd answered truthfully. "For a long time I thought I was God's gift to girls, basketball, and Sweet Valley University." He turned to face her and scratched his head in a gesture of bemusement. "Why am I telling you all this?"

"Because I'm interested."

"Don't you have better things to do than stand around on a beautiful cruise ship listening to a very confused ex–basketball player?"

"No," she said bluntly.

"Why not?" he exclaimed. "According to the brochure in my cabin, this ship's got tennis courts, swimming pools, movie theaters, a beauty shop, clothing boutiques, golf, dance lessons . . ." He trailed off and lifted his hands. "Why aren't you taking advantage of all this luxury?"

"Why aren't you?" she countered.

"Because . . . because . . ." He felt his smile falter. He looked around, staring at the sky and the waves. Finally he met her gaze. "Because I don't have anybody to do those things with," he said in a level voice. "And I've never felt quite so lonely."

She smiled and leaned back, studying his face. "A guy as good looking as you? It's hard to believe you're lonely."

"You'd be surprised," he said.

"Poor baby," she said in an ironic tone, pouting her lips.

That made him laugh. "Why are you giving me a hard time? I just spilled my guts and all you can say is 'poor baby'?"

"I give everybody a hard time," she said with a laugh. "When I think they need it."

"You think I need a hard time?"

"No. Not really," she said in a more serious, gentle voice. "I think you need somebody to play with. Wanna start with skeet and work our way up to the disco? Or just walk around and shoot the breeze?"

"I'd vote for walking around and shooting the breeze."

"So what are we waiting for?" She took his arm and began guiding him toward the engine room. "Tell me, Todd. How do you feel about Clay Meyer at Illinois? Is he going to make it to the pros?"

"Closed!" Jessica moaned, pressing her face against the glass of the ship's Makeover at Sea shop. "How can they be closed already?"

Isabella looked at her watch. "It's almost seven."

Jessica turned and leaned against the door. "How can they do this to me? I can't go to dinner with no makeup. Let's check the lost and found again. Maybe somebody's turned in my makeup case by now."

"It's too late," Isabella said. "You can borrow some makeup from me. I'm sure that Lila, Denise, and I can come up with enough stuff to tide you over until tomorrow. Come on, we'd better get back to our cabins and get ready for dinner. Danny and I are supposed to have dinner with Jason and his fiancée."

"Have you met them?"

"Briefly," Isabella answered. "But then Jason and Danny got to talking and the next thing I knew, they had disappeared. So I came looking for you."

"Thanks a lot," Jessica said in a sour voice.

Isabella laughed. "I didn't mean it that way. And if anybody should have her feelings hurt, it's me. The minute Danny saw Jason, it was like he forgot all about me."

"That doesn't sound good," Jessica said.

Isabella shrugged good-naturedly. "You know how it is when you see an old friend. There are a million things you want to tell them and a million things you want to hear. As soon as they get all their reminiscing out of the way, he'll be more interested in me." She looked around as they stepped from the shopping area onto the outer perimeter of the deck. The sun was setting, and the sky was a pink-and-orange blaze.

Isabella leaned against the rail and smiled serenely. "This is the most romantic place I've ever been."

Jessica frowned and felt a little stab of envy. She wished she felt as self-confident as Isabella. Isabella was beautiful, and she always attracted great guys who fell madly in love with her.

Danny had gone off with a guy friend today, but Isabella wasn't bothered at all. Why? Because she was secure about herself and her relationship with Danny.

"I've always thought a cruise would be the greatest honeymoon," Isabella commented as they turned back toward the stairwell that led down to their cabins. "So getting married right onboard the ship makes perfect sense, doesn't it? I think Danny's friends really came up with a great wedding plan."

Jessica forced her face into a stiff grin. Isabella was usually so tactful, it was strange that she didn't realize how insensitive she was being right now.

Jessica and Mike McAllery had never had a honeymoon. Now, finally, Jessica was taking an incredibly romantic trip—and she was all by herself.

She heard a burst of raucous laughter behind her and looked over her shoulder at a group of kids who were coming down the staircase behind them. OK. So she wasn't exactly all by herself.

Jessica sighed. For the past few months her love life had been a categorical disaster. Unlike Isabella, who always attracted great guys, Jessica had developed an absolute genius for getting involved with one Mr. Wrong after another.

The one guy who appeared to really care about

her—the guy who was her guardian angel—seemed determined to remain in the shadows. But why?

Isabella and Jessica squeezed their way past a knot of people coming up the stairs. Jessica briefly wondered what her chances of meeting somebody onboard were.

Somebody tall, dark, and handsome.

Somebody with a broad set of shoulders.

Somebody like her maddeningly elusive mystery man.

Was it possible that he might be onboard the *Homecoming Queen*?

Tom slapped some aftershave on his freshly shaven cheeks and glanced at the travel clock beside his bed. He couldn't believe it was almost eight o'clock.

He hadn't seen Elizabeth since he'd helped Jessica move into the other cabin. The twins had gone off to explore together, and Elizabeth had promised to be back in her cabin and ready to go to the dining room at seven fifty.

There was a knock on the door, and Tom hurried to open it.

It was Jessica. "Elizabeth asked me to tell you that she'll meet you in the dining room," she said. "She wanted to go get some postcards before dinner."

Tom nodded. "OK." Then he noticed that Jessica was wearing shorts and a T-shirt instead of the casual-formal dress that had been suggested as appropriate for the main dining room. "Aren't you going to dinner?"

Jessica nodded. "Sure. But I'm running late. I had to go trick-or-treating for makeup."

Lila put the finishing touches on her makeup and studied the results with a critical eye. There were still purple circles under her eyes. She'd been crying for the last hour.

She was having a wonderful time. Too good a time. Bruce was a great companion, and she had enjoyed every minute of their time together—starting the second that they'd left campus in the stretch limo that Bruce had hired just for the two of them. In the back they had shared a gourmet breakfast—hot croissants and steaming café au lait.

A stretch limo had met them at the Miami airport, and again they had enjoyed a romantic interlude for two. Lila laughed, remembering Bruce's diplomatic attempts to discourage the others from riding with them.

When they'd arrived at the boat, they had been given full VIP treatment. Everything had been arranged in advance by Bruce. He'd even had fresh lilacs waiting in her cabin.

After checking in and changing clothes, they

had toured the ship, had high tea, and shopped for a few items.

When Lila had returned to her deluxe luxury suite to rest, she suddenly realized that she hadn't thought about Tisiano since last night. The guilt was overwhelming. It seemed almost *sinful* to feel so young and alive when the husband that she had loved was gone.

She shivered. Tisiano had been very superstitious. He'd been careful not to speak ill of the dead, certain that their spirits lingered. Lila had laughed at his superstitions. But now, she couldn't help wondering. . . . There were so many strange tales about the ocean. And Tisiano had died at sea.

The ticking of the clock on the wall suddenly seemed unusually loud. The ocean air howled against the porthole. She opened it to cool the cabin, and a gust of wind blew in. The lights seemed to flicker as Lila hugged her arms. "Tisiano?" she whispered. "Are you there? Can you hear me?"

She stood perfectly still, listening. Was it really possible that Tisiano was with her? Could he be watching her every move? Maybe he felt betrayed by the way she was moving on with her life.

A knock at the door surprised her and she jumped, letting out a startled yell. The door burst open and Bruce hurried in. "What's the matter? Why did you scream?"

She smiled and her shoulders sagged with relief. "The lights flickered, and I got spooked. That's all."

Bruce looked around the room, as if searching for an intruder. "You sure?"

"I'm sure." Lila picked up her bag from the bed and reached for her white silk wrap. "Let's go to dinner. I'm hungry."

She hurriedly shut the door and almost raced down the hall, refusing to turn and look back. She was afraid that if she did, she might encounter a reproachful stare from Tisiano's ghost.

Tom straightened the collar of the crisp white shirt under his navy blazer before striding into the dining room. He couldn't wait to meet Jason and his fiancée.

The misunderstanding with Elizabeth had been a setback. But he was a grown man. He could cope with a little rejection and not get bent out of shape.

He pushed open the swinging double doors and walked in. The elegant dining room was bathed in flickering candlelight. Huge tropical flower arrangements sat in the middle of each table, and every surface gleamed and glittered with silver and crystal.

All the men wore sport coats, and the women had on an array of colorful dresses. In the background a mellow jazz band played soft music. Black-jacketed waiters circulated around the tables, filling water glasses and taking orders for the first course.

Tom's eyes searched the room until he found Danny and Elizabeth. Danny was talking animatedly, leaning over someone to talk to another guy. *That must be Jason,* Tom thought.

He quickened his step and widened his smile as he approached the table. Elizabeth's eyes lit up when she saw him. Isabella's lips curved into a smile of greeting as Danny sat back and grinned. "Tom! Come meet Jason Pierce." Tom leaned across the table and shook hands with Jason, a nice-looking guy about his own height.

"And this is Jason's fiancée, Nicole," Danny added.

"Hello, Tom," said a warm, familiar voice. Tom's eyes turned toward Jason's fiancée and the smile froze on his face.

Chapter
Thirteen

"Remember that guy who always wore the ten-gallon cowboy hat and boots?" Jason said.

"There were two of them!" Danny responded, laughing so hard he was nearly doubled up. "Brothers. One year apart. And neither one of them more than five feet tall."

"They looked like fire hydrants wearing rodeo outfits!" Jason said, slapping his knee.

Isabella's cheeks ached from laughing. Danny had told her that he and Jason had had a lot of funny experiences in high school. And she'd heard a lot of these stories before. But tonight they seemed funnier.

Jason pulled his chair closer to Danny's. "Remember the domino marathon?"

Danny threw back his head and pounded the table. "That was the best, man." He turned to

Tom and began to describe the domino game they'd planned in order to raise money for their high school science lab.

Tom was grinning, and he appeared to be listening. But Isabella couldn't help feeling he wasn't really paying much attention.

Elizabeth had seemed a little stiff when she arrived at dinner, and Isabella had wondered if she and Tom had some kind of argument. But now Elizabeth was laughing at Danny and Jason's stories. Her hand rested on top of Tom's, and her eyes were sparkling. Clearly there wasn't a problem between Elizabeth and Tom.

"Excuse me," a soft-voiced waiter said, removing her dinner plate with its remains of duck, asparagus, and wild rice cooked with mushrooms.

Busboys and waiters moved unobtrusively around the table, removing plates, pouring coffee, and scraping crumbs from the tablecloth. Danny and Jason didn't stop talking for a second. After a few minutes the conversation turned to the current sports scandal at Jason's school.

"You'd never get involved in something like that, would you?" Jason asked Tom.

Tom's mouth was split in a wide smile. And he was watching Jason's face intently. But he didn't respond to the question. Tom blinked when he realized everyone was watching him. "I'm sorry," he said. "I didn't hear you over the rattle of the coffee cups. What was the question?"

"If you knew your teammate had a rival team's playbook, would you tell?" Jason repeated.

"Are we playing Scruples again?"

Danny waved his hand in front of Tom's face. "Are you awake, guy? We're talking about Jason's school. You read about it. It was in all the papers. I'm talking about the kicker who found the playbook for Californian State U and sold copies of it to every team in the conference."

Tom still looked blank.

"You did a television piece on it for the campus station!" Danny reminded him.

Tom pinched the bridge of his nose. "Oh! Oh! Right. Sorry. I was just . . . just . . ." He shrugged. "I must have gotten too much sun today."

Elizabeth pressed her hand affectionately against his cheek. "You'll sleep well tonight," she assured him. "I think we all will."

Isabella watched Tom's eyes rest briefly on Nicole's face and then dart away. Nicole looked stricken. Tom was beet red. And both of them seemed to be looking absolutely everywhere but at each other.

Hmmm. Interesting.

"I think I'll step out on the deck and get some air," Tom said, standing up.

"I'll come with you," Elizabeth offered. She put down her coffee cup.

"No, no," Tom protested. "Stay here and order dessert. I'm just going to cool off a little, and then I'll be back."

"Yeah! Stay and order dessert," Jason urged. "That way I won't feel too bad about having dessert myself." He lifted his hand and signaled to the waiter. "Nicole, honey. You want a dessert?"

"No, thank you," she said quietly.

Danny began to stand. "I think I'll step outside with Tom. I really need to stretch my legs too."

Isabella reached out and caught his hand. She'd been a good sport all night. Now she was ready for a little of Danny's undivided attention. "I've got a better idea. How about stretching your legs on the dance floor?"

"OK," Danny agreed. "Let's go." He took Isabella's hand, and the two of them left Jason and Elizabeth happily debating the relative merits of dark chocolate and milk chocolate.

Isabella felt Danny's arms wrap around her waist, and they began to sway back and forth. "Jason is really nice," she said. "Tons of personality."

Danny chuckled. "Isn't he the greatest? Aside from Tom Watts, he's the only guy in the whole world that I trust one hundred percent."

They turned a bit and Isabella could watch

their table over Danny's broad shoulder. Jason and Elizabeth had ordered a variety of desserts and seemed to be tasting them all. Beside Jason, Nicole sat with a stiff back and a forced smile.

When Danny pressed his cheek against hers, Isabella decided to forget about everything but the warmth of her boyfriend's arms. Her eyelids lowered blissfully, but from underneath her dark lashes, she saw Nicole excuse herself and make her way toward the exit.

"Tom!" she said in a low voice.

Tom turned and saw her standing on the deck, silhouetted against the moon with her gauzy wrap floating around her shoulders. The tendrils of her dark hair blew around her face, creating a halo.

"Aside from the engagement ring, you look exactly the way you looked the last time I saw you," he said, thrusting his hands into his pockets. "The night we went dancing."

She stepped forward, and Tom saw her dark eyes and high cheekbones. "I thought maybe you'd forgotten me," she said.

"I thought *you'd* forgotten *me*," he countered.

"I didn't forget you." She turned her face away and bit her lip uncertainly. "I guess you wonder why I never returned your phone calls after our last date," she said after a long and awkward pause.

"Yeah. I wondered." Tom lifted his chin slightly, feeling defensive. Nicole Riley and he had dated several times the summer after their senior year in high school. There had been some good chemistry between them. But then she'd pulled away and never done him the courtesy of telling him why.

At the time, it had hurt his feelings. He'd gotten over it fairly quickly. But it had been difficult to take a slosh of cold water in the face and never find out what he'd done wrong. It was a long time ago, but it still rankled.

"I went to visit some friends, met Jason, and fell in love," she said simply. "I couldn't think about anybody or anything else. That's why I ended up going to CSU."

"Why didn't you just tell me?"

She shook her head. "I was a coward. It would have been an uncomfortable conversation, and I didn't feel like dealing with it." She looked back toward the dining room. "Let me ask you a question. When we met at dinner, why did you act like you didn't know me?"

Tom's mouth fell open a bit and he took an uneasy step back. "I don't know," he said truthfully.

"It would have been uncomfortable," she said with a laugh. "Just like the summer after our senior year. I kept meaning to call you. But once the time for true confessions had passed, I felt like I *couldn't* tell you, because then you'd wonder why I hadn't told you before. And Jason would wonder why I hadn't told *him* about *you*, and . . ." She threw out her hands. "What can I say? It got complicated."

"I think things have gotten complicated again," Tom said, biting the inside of his cheek and staring up at the sky.

"Meaning?"

"Meaning honesty is a great thing. But so is timing. And I think that . . . uh . . . well . . ." He laughed nervously. "I think if we were going to say anything about knowing each other, we should have done it at the table. Because *now* if we say anything . . ."

". . . they'll wonder why we didn't say anything right off."

"Exactly."

"And it'll make it seem like there was more between us than there really was."

"Right."

"So it should be our secret."

Tom nodded slowly. "Right."

"OK by me," she said agreeably.

Tom smiled and relaxed. He'd forgotten how likable Nicole was. "Aren't you a little young to be getting married?" he asked, changing the subject.

"Everybody seems to think so."

"This is OK with your folks?"

"They know by now that it's pretty impossible to stop me once I've made up my mind to do something. I'm ready to get married. So is Jason." She grinned mischievously. "And so are our ten bridesmaids."

Tom laughed. *"Ten!"*

She shrugged. "Hey! I make friends easily. If I asked one, I had to ask them all."

"So how many people are on this ship for your wedding?"

"About fifty," she answered.

"Fifty?"

Nicole nodded. "Yep! Fifty of our closest friends. No families. Jason's dad works for an oil company, and his parents were transferred to Russia last year. My parents said their wedding had been all old folks and relatives—so they just sent us a big check to cover expenses and told us to elope. And that's what we're doing."

"With fifty of your closest friends?" he joked.

"Fifty-one," she said significantly, threading her arm through his. "I'm glad you're here," she added softly. "Will you forgive me? I don't know if I can get married with a clear conscience if you won't. You've sort of lingered in my mind as un-finished business."

Tom patted her hand. "It's all in the past, Nicole. I quit being angry a long time ago. I'm

141

glad you're happy. And I'm looking forward to the wedding." He paused. "Ready to go back in?"

"I'll go in first," she said, moving across the deck. "You wait a few minutes and then follow me."

"See you in the dining room," he said, watching her walk away and feeling as if the situation had been resolved.

"There you are!" Elizabeth called from the door.

Elizabeth appeared on the deck. Her blond hair swished around her shoulders and her pale-pink sheath set off her beautiful shape to perfection. She lifted her face, letting the moonlight fall across it. "It's cooler out here," she said, opening her arms and leaning toward him.

Tom bent down and kissed her neck. Elizabeth was different from Nicole in every way. In a million years, he couldn't imagine Elizabeth rejecting him the way Nicole had. Just freezing him out of her life.

He and Elizabeth were made for each other. He tightened his grasp around her waist. "Elizabeth, I love you."

"I love you too," she murmured.

"Let's go inside and dance," he whispered.

"Let's dance tomorrow night," she whispered back. "Right now, I sort of feel like I need to be with Jess."

"Jessica?" Tom released Elizabeth. "You want to be with Jessica? Now?"

"I think she's a little down in the dumps," Elizabeth said. "Everybody's part of a romantic twosome except for her."

Tom fought to keep his voice calm. "Liz, I know I goofed up on the sleeping arrangements, but aren't we going to spend any time together at all? I mean, I can understand why you don't want to sleep with me, but now you don't even want to dance with me?"

"Tom! You're overreacting."

"No, I'm not," he argued. "You said you wanted us to have some time alone together. When, exactly, do you think that time might be?"

Elizabeth's face darkened. "Tom. You know how much I want us to be together—but Jessica's my sister."

"And I'm your boyfriend. *Your* boyfriend. Not Jessica's."

"I can't believe you're being so childish. How can you make me choose between Jessica and you?"

"Nobody's asking you to choose," he snapped angrily. "I'm just asking you to spend some time with me. What's the point of being on this cruise if we're not going to be together?"

He couldn't believe he was getting rejected again. *Why do I keep setting myself up for this?* "I'll see you later," he said, turning on his heel to walk away.

"Where are you going?" she called.

He came to a stop and turned. "Look. I just need to be alone for a while," he said.

Elizabeth lifted her chin. "Fine. As far as I'm concerned you can be alone for the rest of the cruise." She stalked away.

Tom beat his fist against his thigh in frustration. Great! Now they were officially in a fight. This was not what he had been trying to achieve. He'd wanted to draw her nearer, and he'd wound up pushing her away.

He wondered if he should go after her, then decided against it. He needed to cool off before he said something he would regret.

"What am I talking about?" he muttered unhappily. "I *already* said things I regret."

Why did Nicole have to be the girl Jason was marrying? He wished she weren't on the boat. Seeing her had shaken him up and made him feel insecure. And feeling like that had caused him to pressure Elizabeth.

Now he felt terrible. He pictured Jessica's unhappy face and felt a pang. He didn't want to put Elizabeth in a position where she had to choose between them. "Ohhhh," he groaned out loud. Jessica had been through some rough times. She needed Elizabeth. She needed Tom, too.

He'd have to apologize to Elizabeth. He'd acted like a selfish jerk. Tom swept back his hair, remembering the dark look on her face. She'd looked pretty mad. It would probably be a good idea to give her a little time to calm down.

Maybe the best thing to do was blow off a little steam at the pool table or something. He could swing by Elizabeth's cabin later with some flowers.

Yeah. That was a good plan.

Elizabeth strode angrily back to the table. She'd find Jessica and maybe the two of them could take in a movie or visit some of the shops.

Inside the dining room her eyes swept the tables, searching for Jessica. She saw Winston and Denise sitting with some people who were part of Jason and Nicole's entourage.

Then she saw Todd—looking happier than he had in weeks. He was talking to a pretty Asian girl who seemed to be very interested in what he was saying.

Isabella and Danny were dancing. And so were Jason and Nicole. Lila and Bruce seemed to be doing their personal version of the tango, while Nina and some guy Elizabeth didn't recognize waltzed gracefully around the dance floor.

Unfortunately, Jessica was nowhere to be seen. Elizabeth hurried from the dining room, feeling angry at herself and angry at Tom. Why did he think that his needs had to come first? Why couldn't he understand what a tough position she was in?

And why couldn't she find a way to be there for both her sister and her boyfriend?

Chapter Fourteen

"*Why* did I eat that?" Winston groaned.

"You said you weren't hungry when we went in," Denise marveled. "*How* did you eat so much? Four lobsters! I've never seen anybody eat four lobsters."

Winston laid a hand on his chest and grimaced. "What can I say? I saw the bib, the tank, the waiters. I get around these all-you-can-eat setups and I lose my head."

"All you can eat?" Denise scoffed. "Show a little class, Win. This isn't Saturday night at the cafeteria."

Winston groaned again.

Denise spread the skirt of her vintage cocktail dress and executed a graceful pirouette. "We've done the fine dining."

"I'll say."

"Now we can either dance to the soft music in the dining room or boogie down in the upper-deck disco."

Winston loosened the cummerbund of his forties-style tux as they passed a row of deck chairs. His knees buckled and he sat, feeling his eyes glaze over.

"Winston!" Denise cried, kneeling beside him. "What's wrong?"

Winston wet his lips and swallowed. "I think . . ."

Denise waited.

"I think . . ."

He closed his eyes and swayed slightly. The aluminum frame of the deck chair made an ominous creak.

"Winston! What is it? You're scaring me."

"I think I'm seasick," he whispered.

Jessica went over to the porthole and stared gloomily out at the dark ocean. She'd been excited going in to dinner, but by the end of dessert, she'd felt depressed. She'd been seated next to a really cute guy from Florida State. Naturally the girl sitting on the other side of him was his girlfriend.

They had both been friendly, and the people at her table had insisted that she join them in the disco for some after-dinner dancing. Jessica had agreed to go, but she wasn't looking forward to it.

Everybody would probably have a ready-made dance partner—except her. Then again, she *was* Jessica Wakefield. There might be a hundred guys thrilled at the chance to show her a good time.

Jessica went over to the bureau and frowned down at the jumble of foraged makeup items. There was a green eyeliner that looked hideous on her. And a blush with way too much orange in it. Denise had loaned her a lipstick that was sort of grape colored. And she had a foundation from Isabella that was completely the wrong shade. Jessica made a face when she turned on the overhead light to get a better view of herself. Isabella had ivory skin, and her pale foundation made Jessica's skin look like it was caked with stage makeup.

Jessica reached for a Kleenex in the enamel tissue holder provided by the ship. Like everything else in the cabin, it was elegant.

As she blotted at her face with the tissue, Jessica could hear soft music from the dining room echoing from the upper deck through the window. If only there were someone special to share this trip with. If only her relationship with Mike hadn't been so disastrous, and James Montgomery hadn't been such a jerk. . . . She wiped at her chin with increasing frustration.

"Darn," she muttered. No matter how hard Jessica rubbed, she couldn't seem to erase the obvious foundation line that ran along her jaw. She rubbed even harder, then threw the Kleenex down in disgust.

A loud buzzing sound made her jump. What was it? Then she heard the buzzing twice in rapid succession.

She stepped back from the mirror and looked around for a telephone to answer. There wasn't one. Had an alarm clock gone off by mistake?

Another loud, insistent buzz was followed by a knock. Jessica smiled. She went to the door. "I'm coming!" she shouted. "I didn't realize we had doorbells—" She broke off when she saw a ship's porter standing in the hallway holding a familiar-looking small case and a vase spilling over with red roses.

"Ms. Wakefield?" he inquired. The porter smiled and held up the bag. "I was asked to deliver these things to your cabin. Where would you like me to put them?"

Jessica was too astonished to do anything but step back and allow the porter to pass. Inside the cabin, he looked quickly around, then carefully placed the small case on the bureau and positioned the flower vase on the desk. He stood back, viewed the roses with a critical eye, then plucked at a few of the stems until the arrangement met with his satisfaction. He turned to Jessica and smiled. "Is there anything else I can do?"

Jessica just shook her head, still struggling for words. She reached quickly for her small evening purse so she could give him a tip.

He held up his hand. "No gratuity, please. It's been taken care of. Good night." The porter backed out of the cabin and softly closed the door behind him.

Jessica stood rooted to the floor, her mind racing. Who had retrieved her makeup case? And who was sending her flowers? She dove forward, searching frantically through the bouquet for a card.

When she saw there wasn't one, she knew exactly who had retrieved her makeup case and sent her flowers. Her guardian angel had struck again. Her mystery man was on the ship!

She drew in her breath with a gasp. Maybe he was waiting in the hall, watching to be sure that his gift had been properly delivered.

Jessica swung open the door and stuck her head into the hallway. She looked to the left and saw nothing but a long expanse of red carpet, lit with soft yellow bulbs set in brass sconces mounted along the wall.

But when she looked to the right, she saw a tall back and a wide set of shoulders disappear around the corner that led to the stairs. "Wait!" she cried. "Please, wait!"

She ran outside the cabin, letting the door shut

behind her. Her high heels wobbled slightly as she hurried to catch up. Her heart was racing with excitement.

"Wait!" she cried, hearing footsteps clanging on the metal stairwell that led to the upper deck. "Wait!"

She grabbed the rail and began climbing the stairs herself. One of her heels caught on the edge of a stair, but she stepped right out of it and kicked the other one off so she could run faster.

She didn't care about her shoes anymore. Or her makeup case. Or anything else. All she wanted was a look at the man who had devoted himself to protecting her for the past several weeks. A man who obviously cared very much about her.

She stepped out on the open deck that formed the perimeter of the disco. Inside the club, she could see people dancing and hear music playing. But she seemed to be the only person on the deck.

Her eye caught the movement of a shadow several yards away. A figure was there. She was sure of it. "Hello?" she said quietly, starting toward it. "Is someone there?"

She heard a clattering sound as the figure bumped against some equipment. And then he was running again, taking the stairs that led to the next deck.

Why was her mystery man was so determined to remain mysterious? Was he afraid his looks might repel her? Whatever he looked like, Jessica was consumed with curiosity. "Whoever you are," she called. "Please don't run away!"

But the footsteps continued.

"Please! Wait!" She broke into a run, determined to follow him no matter how many decks she had to pursue him across. As she neared the stairs, her foot hit a puddle. The next thing she knew she was skidding across the slippery, polished deck on the silky fabric of her stockings.

The skirt of her dress blew up and obscured her vision. She felt the rail of the ship against her stomach as she tumbled over it. "Oh, my God!" she cried. "I'm *falliiiiing*!"

"How about some clear soup?" the ship's nurse asked brightly.

Bryan looked at the large expanse of stainless steel tray. A small plastic cup of broth sat dead center. "That's it? That's all I can have?"

Nurse Higgins set the tray down next to the reclining chair in which Bryan sat dolefully watching a movie on the infirmary's VCR. Their selection of videos was pretty limited. They had exactly one—*Sleeping Beauty*.

"I'm starving," he complained.

"We'll bring you a nice big breakfast tomorrow morning," she assured him. "Assuming you have a good night."

Bryan sat up straight and threw off the soft, woolly afghan that covered his legs. They had given him some paper slippers to keep his feet warm, and a regal *Homecoming Queen* crest adorned each toe. "You mean I'm supposed to stay here all night?"

The nurse gently pushed him back into his seat. She didn't have to push hard. At six feet and at least two hundred pounds, she looked like a gray-haired linebacker in a white polyester dress. "Doctor's orders," she reminded him sweetly. "You've had a pretty major blow to the head, stitches, and you've never been on a boat before. The first day out can be a bit hard on the system. Under the circumstances, it's best to stick to clear liquids. You don't want to be ill."

"Where is he?" Bryan demanded. "I want to talk to him right now about getting out of here."

"Now, Mr. Nelson," the nurse began in an entirely different tone. "I have my orders and I intend to follow them." She seemed to have abandoned all pretense of humoring him.

Bryan tried to sit up. "I'm a grown man and I—"

"Don't be foolish!" she snapped, placing a hand on his chest and shoving hard.

"Oommph!" he wheezed, falling back into his recliner.

"Now drink your soup and let's not have any

more nonsense." She turned and walked away, disappearing behind a swinging door into the dispensary.

Bryan picked up the soup and stared right through it to the bottom of the round cup. This soup was clear, all right. It looked like water with an oily sheen on top. Not a noodle, vegetable, or bit of chicken in sight.

Delicious smells from the dining room wafted in through the ventilating system, and Bryan's stomach rumbled unhappily. He'd known this cruise was going to be a disaster. But in his worst nightmares he hadn't expected anyone to starve him to death.

He heard a glittery laugh outside the infirmary. He turned his gloomy gaze toward the door just in time to watch Nina float in on Dr. Daniels's arm. "Oh, Bryan," she breathed. "You're not going to believe what we had for dinner."

"We?" he repeated dryly.

Apparently his sarcasm was lost on Nina, because she didn't pause before launching into a recitation of each of the five courses she'd eaten.

"Hmmm," he grunted, lifting his pathetic cup of broth to his lips.

"Not too much," Dr. Daniels cautioned, taking the cup from Bryan's hand.

"But . . ." Bryan began.

"Now, now. I know we think we can just gulp down as much soup as we want," Dr. Daniels said in an offensively avuncular manner. "But it's unwise. Trust me. I know. I'm a *doctor*."

Bryan ground his teeth. At this rate, the guy was going to be patting him on the head and offering him a balloon.

Nina seemed to noticed the pained look on his face, and her expression immediately changed from amusement to concern. "What's the matter, Bryan? Does your head hurt?"

Bryan took a deep breath. It was time to say what was on his mind. He was sick of being treated like a pesky child. And he was sick of being on this lousy ship. He wanted to let her know, in no uncertain terms, that as far as he was concerned this whole cruise thing was a washout.

Short of sinking, he couldn't see how things could get any worse.

The door to the infirmary flew open and Winston stood there, his mouth opening and closing like a fish's. Denise stood behind him, wringing her hands. "Is there a doctor here?" he wailed.

"Winston! What's wrong?" Nina gasped.

"I'm seasick!" Winston cried, diving forward.

"Nurse Higgins!" Dr. Daniels shouted, lunging toward the counter and grabbing for a stainless steel basin.

But he was too late. Bryan saw it coming, but he was powerless to save himself.

Winston Egbert clutched his stomach, moaned like a man in the last stages of an agonizing illness, and then threw up right on top of Bryan's head.

Chapter
Fifteen

The water around Jessica was warm. It almost felt like a caress. Her arms floated limply and her legs were heavy but oddly buoyant. She felt as if she were being carried through the air by an angel.

A large hand smoothed her hair with a loving touch. "Don't leave me," she wanted to say, closing her fingers over the breast of his shirt.

But she couldn't make her lips move. She was asleep. And drifting deeper into slumber.

Bryan caught a glimpse of himself in the mirror. He looked so angry, he even scared himself. His eyes were blazing, and his lips were pressed so tightly together they looked like a crack in a block of stone.

"Bryan?" Nina said softly. "Why do you have your fists balled so tight?"

"I'm bracing myself," he answered.

"For what?"

"For when we hit the iceberg!"

"Now stop that kind of talk," Nurse Higgins ordered, coming in with a pile of fresh towels. A separate area had been partitioned off with a curtain, and from the other side, they heard Winston groan loudly. Nurse Higgins shook her head and looked pointedly at Bryan. "See what comes from eating too heavily on your first day at sea?"

Bryan tried to open his mouth and protest that he hadn't eaten *at all*, but it was too much trouble. His teeth were clenched so tightly together it felt like his jaw muscles were locked.

Nurse Higgins reached for a garbage can lined with a plastic bag. "Now, then. Let's get you out of those clothes and into the infirmary shower. Then we'll find you a nightgown—"

"Night*gown*! Don't you have any pajamas?" Bryan asked.

"This is like the hospital, Bryan," Nina said softly. "Everybody in a hospital wears a nightgown."

Nurse Higgins twirled her fingers, signaling Nina to turn around so she could strip the vomit-strewn clothes from Bryan. "There are no icebergs in the Caribbean," she said, efficiently helping him remove his shirt and pants and dropping them into the hamper. "And even if there were . . . this ship is built to exceed all known safety standards. We haven't lost a passenger yet."

"Passenger overboard!" shouted a voice in the distance.

A guy Bryan recognized from Sweet Valley University stuck his head into the infirmary. "We need the doctor on deck. Now. They just fished somebody out of the water. And it looks like she's dead."

Nina raced out, and Dr. Daniels hurtled from behind the curtain. He unceremoniously pushed past Bryan, followed by Nurse Higgins.

Moments later Bryan stood alone in the middle of the infirmary. He was wearing nothing but his underwear, and he was cold and hungry.

He was also scared to death.

"Come on, Jessica. Wake up!" a voice ordered.

Jessica refused to answer. She didn't want to wake up; she was too sleepy.

"Can you hear me? Wake up."

The pillow beneath her head was hard. And so was the mattress. It didn't feel like her bed at all.

"Jessica!" The voice was more insistent now.

There's a reason I don't want to wake up, she thought. *What is it?* Then she remembered. When she opened her eyes, the angel would be gone. And she didn't want him to be gone. She didn't want to be alone anymore.

"Jessica!" the voice urged. "I know you can hear me. Now come on. Open your eyes."

A hand gently slapped at her cheeks, and Jessica angrily turned her head away. "Stop that," she muttered. Her eyes popped open and she saw frightened faces crowded around her. Then she heard a collective sigh of relief.

"Is she OK?" somebody asked from the edge of the circle.

"I think so," someone else answered.

The crowd began to shift uneasily. "Jess," she heard Elizabeth sob. She turned her head and saw her sister kneeling beside her, her eyes large with terror. Tears streamed down her face.

"What's the matter, Lizzie?" Jessica asked in a raspy voice, realizing as she spoke that her lungs felt raw, as if she were recovering from a bad cough. "What happened to you?"

She saw the attractive ship's doctor sit back on his heels, sigh, and wipe his brow on the sleeve of his white shirt. "Let's spread out and give her some air," he suggested to the crowd.

The crowd dispersed, leaving Jessica, Elizabeth, and the doctor.

Jessica saw Nina and Denise back away. "We're right here if you need us," Nina assured Elizabeth in a low tone.

The doctor leaned over Jessica and spoke. "I'm Dr. Daniels. You're going to be fine. But the nurse

161

has gone to get a gurney. Just lie here until it arrives. Then we'll wheel you to the infirmary. Your legs are probably a little shaky after what happened."

"What did happen?" she asked Elizabeth as the doctor stood and walked away a few steps to confer with someone else.

"You fell overboard," Elizabeth said softly.

Jessica's heart gave a sickening thump. Now she knew now why her mattress was so hard. She was lying on the deck of the ship.

"How did it happen?"

Elizabeth shook her head in bewilderment. "I don't know. All I know is that suddenly people were screaming that somebody had just pulled a body from the water. Then when I got on deck, I realized it was—" She broke off, choking.

A series of memories came flooding back to Jessica so clearly, they burst behind her eyes like a Technicolor slide show.

She saw an image—the makeup case. A vase of bright red roses. Then she remembered the tall figure with the broad shoulders.

"You said somebody pulled me from the water?" Jessica asked quickly. "Did you see who?"

Elizabeth shook her head. "No. All I know is that somebody pumped the water out of your lungs and gave you mouth to mouth. By the time

I got here, the doctor and a whole bunch of other people were surrounding you."

"But who rescued me?" Jessica persisted. "Who jumped into the water and pulled me out?"

Elizabeth took her hand. "I'm sure we'll find out when the commotion dies down."

Bryan buttoned himself into Nurse Higgins's size-eighteen white polyester nursing dress. He'd searched everywhere for a paper gown, but the supply closet had been locked. The only thing he'd found to wear was her spare uniform, which hung on a hook on the back of the closet door.

From behind the curtain Winston whimpered. "I'm dying," he heard Winston whisper hoarsely.

Bryan fought the urge to feel sorry for him. Winston sounded awful, but he deserved it.

"Water," Winston croaked like a man lost in the desert. "Water, please. Won't somebody bring me some water?"

Bryan rolled his eyes. Denise had run out of the infirmary along with everybody else when the cry had sounded. Just thinking about being underwater made Bryan's chest feel tight and claustrophobic. Who had fallen? And would they be all right?

"Water," he heard Winston croak again.

No matter how angry he was with Egbert, Bryan couldn't deny a sick man a sip of water.

That probably violated some kind of human rights law.

He walked over to the stainless steel lavatory and filled a paper cup with water. He turned and started toward the curtain, then paused. If he went inside that cubicle, Winston would see him in a dress.

"Ohhhhhh," Winston groaned.

On second thought, Winston wasn't in any shape to notice somebody's clothes.

Feeling completely ridiculous, Bryan stepped into the cubicle and recoiled when he saw Winston's face. He'd heard about people having green faces, but he'd never really believed it. Winston looked green all right. And his usually faint freckles stood out like bright polka dots. "I brought you some water," Bryan said, trying to make his voice sound kind and comforting.

Winston sat up slightly and stared at Bryan with dull and listless eyes. Then he fell back limply against the pillows, giggling helplessly.

"Knock it off, Egbert! Do you want the water or not?"

But the only response was another weak burst of laughter.

"OK. Fine. You drink it when you're ready. I'm out of here." Bryan slammed the cup down on the little bedside table. He didn't care what Dr. Daniels or the nurse said, he was spending the night in his own cabin, as far away as possible from Winston Egbert.

He thrust the curtain aside and stormed out just as Dr. Daniels and Nurse Higgins came rushing in with a gurney. Behind them were Elizabeth, Denise, and Nina.

Nina drew in her breath with a gasp. Her eyes widened and her fingers flew to her mouth. Then her shoulders began to shake with laughter. Everybody else was quick to join in, although Elizabeth seemed to made a weak attempt to suppress her high-pitched giggles.

Bryan could feel every pair of eyes on him, taking it all in—a tall, well-built black man wearing a size-eighteen polyester dress.

He'd have to break up with Nina, of course. There was no way they could go on after this. She'd never take him seriously again. And he'd have to change schools.

Having done that, he'd be all right. Nobody would ever have to know. It would just be a rumor. Something he could deny as an ugly racist accusation if it were ever raised later in his career. *Me in a dress? You've got to be kidding! Man, those folks will do anything to discredit a black man!*

"Oh, thank goodness I'm prepared," Denise gasped between giggles. She removed a camera from her pocket.

Bryan groaned, but he was too stunned and

horrified to respond. Once again he was powerless to save himself. He could only stand paralyzed, like a deer caught in headlights.

"Say cheese!" Denise instructed before snapping the picture and recording for posterity the most humiliating moment of Bryan Nelson's whole life.

"OK, now," the nurse said briskly. "Let's take off that wet sweater." She pulled Jessica's wet mohair top up over her head and tugged slightly. "Open your fist, dear, I can't get the sleeve off."

For the first time Jessica realized that her hand was clutched tightly into a ball. She'd been making a fist ever since she'd regained consciousness. She opened her hand and something fell to the floor with a plinking sound.

"I'm sorry," the nurse said. "There goes one of your buttons." She set the sweater aside, leaned over, and picked up the button.

"May I see that?" Jessica asked.

The nurse smiled and placed the button in the palm of her hand. Jessica knew immediately that it hadn't come from her sweater. The button was round and white and looked as if it had been carved out of bone. It was a button from a shirt. A man's shirt.

Don't leave me, she had tried to whisper, clutching at his shirt.

Jessica closed her fingers over the button and held it to her heart. Finally she had a clue. "If only you could speak," she whispered. "If only you could tell me who my guardian angel is."

Tom ran up the bowling lane, taking three long strides. He let the ball go, and it rolled smoothly down the highly polished alley. It hit the pins and knocked them all over with a loud and satisfying rumble that reverberated through the whole bowling alley.

Danny came over and slapped him on the back. "Thank you, Watts. The SVU side needed that."

"If CSU gave you a bowling scholarship, could we convince you to transfer?" Jason asked Tom.

"CSU doesn't give bowling scholarships," one of Jason's friends pointed out.

"What! No bowling scholarships? I'm scandalized. It's the sport of kings."

After his argument with Elizabeth, Tom had gone to the pool room. He'd already shot a few games by himself when Danny, Jason, and a few other guys had wandered in and decided to head for the bowling alley. The SVU group had immediately formed a team and challenged Jason and his friends to a match.

Every different level of bowling expertise, or lack thereof, was represented on the two teams. They had rank beginners and old pros. The mix had produced a lot of ups and downs in the score.

"Way to go!" Jason whistled his approval as one of his teammates sent the ball thundering down the gutter.

"I missed every pin," the bowler protested, hanging his head in mock chagrin. "Why are you applauding?"

"Because it was so much fun to watch," Jason said. "Come on. Let's all give Lester a hand."

Everybody on both teams began to applaud and cheer wildly.

Tom reached for his soda and grinned. Danny had been right about Jason. He was a great guy, and he got along well with everybody. He had a nice bunch of friends, too. Tom envied Jason slightly. It was probably fun to have a big group of friends to hang out with.

Tom and Danny were best friends. But they were both loners and had been partners in isolation for much of their first year of college. They did almost everything together. Not only because they enjoyed each other's company, but also because neither one of them had many other friends.

Both of them had had an emotionally grueling freshman year, and they'd bonded like brothers. Tom couldn't imagine life without Danny now. He was the only person, besides Elizabeth, that he completely trusted.

And vice versa. Danny had a much more outgoing personality than Tom. And he was more at ease with new people. But Tom knew that deep down, Danny was slow to trust.

Jason got up, took a ball, and then began an elaborate bowling walk that made them all laugh. When he got a strike, he dusted off his hands. "That's our game."

"OK! That's it. I'm going to bed." Lester reached for his jacket, and a couple of the other guys nodded and began stretching and yawning.

"Oh, come on," Jason protested. "The night is young. It's only—" He looked at his watch and grimaced. "OK, so it's late," he agreed. "But this is what vacations are for. Right? Staying up late. Having a good time."

"If I don't go to bed now," Lester announced, "I'll sleep away the rest of the cruise."

"Me too," Danny said. "I'm calling it a night. Tom? You ready to turn in?"

Tom reached for his jacket and loafers. "I'm ready. But I've got something I need to do first. I want to say good night to Elizabeth."

And apologize for being an idiot. He'd forgotten to get the flowers, and by now the florist was closed. But he'd pour on the charm tonight and surprise her with a dozen yellow roses in the morning.

Tom waved good night after quickly returning his bowling shoes. He hurried in the direction of

Elizabeth's cabin. Whatever she and Jessica had done tonight, it had probably been relaxing. He hoped she would be receptive to an apology *and* a few minutes of passionate good-night kissing in the moonlight.

He had to climb two flights of steps to get to Elizabeth's cabin. The hallway was warm, and the light was low and mellow. When he reached her door, he lifted his fist and knocked softly.

The door opened and Elizabeth peered out.

Tom gave her his most seductive smile. "I was thinking that now might be a good time to pry you away from Jessica for a bit and . . ."

"Tom!" Elizabeth interrupted in an outraged tone. "I can't believe you! I can't think of a worse time."

Elizabeth slammed the door. Tom stood motionless in front of it, his mouth hanging open. Finally he stepped back, infuriated. How dare she slam the door in his face?

"Looks like we're both destined to be lonely tonight."

He whirled and saw Nicole leaning against the wall beneath a brass lighting fixture. "Nicole! How long have you been standing there?"

"Long enough to hear you get your head bitten off. Is she always that short tempered? Or just after her sister nearly drowns?"

"Nearly drowns? What are you talking about?"

"Her sister fell overboard. Somebody saved her—but just barely. I saw him giving her mouth to mouth. It looked like she was dead, and I—" She broke off and tried to compose herself. "She's going to be OK. At least I think so. She was sitting up and talking. But it was pretty . . ."

Nicole's lips began to tremble, and her long black eyelashes glittered as tears collected on the tips. "It was really unnerving," she finished with a choke, her shoulders drooping.

Instinctively Tom reached for her, pulling her close. "No wonder Elizabeth was so weird. And no wonder you're upset. Why didn't somebody come get me? Or Jason?"

"Nobody knew where you were. Or Jason either," she added bitterly. "I know he loves me," she said. "But sometimes I swear he'd rather be with his friends than with me. He's always off somewhere with his pals when I need him." She began to sob silently, and Tom pressed her face into his shoulder and laid his cheek on top of her hair.

"Don't cry," he soothed.

"I'm so glad you're here," she said with a sniffle.

"I know," he whispered.

"I'd forgotten how comforting you are. You make everything seem like it's going to be OK."

Tom smiled. The woman he *should* be comforting

had just slammed the door in his face and stomped on his already-fragile ego. It was nice having someone appreciate his presence—even if it was a girl who had never returned his phone calls.

"I feel so awful about what happened."

"She'll be OK," Tom said. "If she was sitting up and talking, those are pretty good indicators that—"

"I mean about what happened between us."

"Oh!"

Her arms tightened around him, and she turned her tear-streaked face up toward him. The soft glow from the lamps in the hallway made her porcelain skin look as if she were carved from ivory.

He'd almost forgotten how heartbreakingly beautiful she was. She felt fragile in his arms, and he loved the way she delicately clung to his neck. "Nicole," he began, his breath suddenly ragged.

Her lips whispered his name, and she stared at him as if she were seeing him for the very first time. Involuntarily he began to bend his head toward hers.

A door opened down the hall, and they guiltily broke apart. Tom's heart was beating hard inside his chest. He coughed, trying to cover up his uneven breathing.

Nicole swayed slightly on wobbly legs; she hid her flustered face by pretending to arrange her hair.

172

A girl Tom didn't recognize came hurrying down the hall. She smiled as she passed by, then disappeared into another cabin.

Tom and Nicole each took a step away from the other. "I think we should try to stay as far apart as possible," he said.

She nodded, her head bobbing quickly up and down. "Right. Right."

"I don't think we should talk, or touch, or . . ."

"I agree," she said hastily, turning away in embarrassment. "I'll see you around." She ran down the hall and raced up the stairs.

Tom's eyes lingered on the stairwell long after she had disappeared. He hated himself for admiring her slender ankles and shapely calves as they disappeared out of sight.

Chapter
Sixteen

"I'm sorry," Elizabeth said for the fifteenth time. "You're right. I misunderstood, and I should never have slammed the door in your face. I apologize profusely." She gave Tom her brightest smile—the one she knew he could never resist. "Now will you please quit sulking?"

"I'm not sulking." He leaned over her shoulder, pushing open the dining room door for her.

"OK. Pouting," she corrected, stepping inside the elegant breakfast room.

"I'm not pouting either. I'm hurt and justifiably angry and—"

"OK, *OK*," Elizabeth teased, shaking his arm as they approached the breakfast buffet. "I said I was sorry. Enough already. I'd had a rough night. I wasn't thinking too clearly. It's not every night your identical twin has a near-death experience.

It's kind of like having one yourself."

"I know," Tom said quickly. He hugged her shoulders. "How's Jessica this morning? Recovered?"

"Fully recovered. And happier than ever," Elizabeth answered. "She says she's up for sight-seeing and shopping."

As the breakfast buffet line moved forward and they stepped up to the long, white-skirted table, Tom took a china plate, decorated with the ship's crest in the center, and politely handed it to Elizabeth. Then he took an even bigger plate for himself.

"Yum," she commented, surveying the food choices. There were five different kinds of muffins. She also saw Danish pastries, eggs Benedict, bacon, sausage, a fried ham. On the other end of the table were platters of hashed-brown potatoes, an array of dried cereal, and heaping bowls of fruit. "Who in the world is going to eat all this?" she inquired in an awed voice.

"I am," Tom answered with a laugh. "At least, I'm going to give it the old college try."

Elizabeth looked over and began to laugh too. Tom's plate was completely full and he wasn't even halfway down the buffet line. "Watch out," she warned as he reached out to take another muffin. "You don't want to wind up like Winston, do you?"

Tom withdrew his hand. "Good point. Besides, I don't have any more room on my plate. I'll have to eat this first and then come back for more," he said.

Elizabeth couldn't resist adding another blueberry muffin to her own plate. *Everybody deserves extra calories on vacation,* she reasoned.

"Come on," Tom said, grabbing a glass of juice. "There's Danny and Isabella. Let's go sit with them." Elizabeth followed Tom to a large round table, where Danny and Isabella sat sipping steaming cups of coffee.

Isabella half stood when she saw Elizabeth. "Liz! How's Jess feeling? We were just talking about her."

"She's fine," Elizabeth assured them. "She's in our cabin right now, changing into her fourth outfit and making out a shopping list for when we get to the island."

The first port of call was a tiny island called St. Lucia. It was famous for its shopping, its quaint architecture, its fish market, and its charm. And the island's shops supposedly had the best bargains on crystal and perfumes in the Caribbean.

"I hope a lifejacket is on Jessica's list. Bryan's too." Isabella looked around and raised her eyebrows. "Dr. Daniels must be a miracle man. Look who else is up and at 'em." She lifted her hand and began to wave.

Winston and Denise were just leaving the buffet line. When they caught sight of Isabella's waving hand, they started in their direction.

"You're alive and well!" Danny commented in surprise as Winston and Denise put their plates down on the table.

"He's alive and eating," Denise said. "I'm trying to convince him that it's probably not a great idea." She adjusted the yellow kerchief she wore over her hair. It perfectly matched the bright yellow beads that formed a sunflower pattern on her strapless dress. Her smooth shoulders were already a golden brown from yesterday's sun.

"You might want to take it easy," Tom said to Winston.

"Yeah, start with something light, like fruit, and work your way up to . . ." Danny frowned at Winston's plate. "What *is* that, anyway?"

"Kidneys," Winston answered, putting a large forkful into his mouth.

"Yuck!" the group groaned.

"I appreciate your concern," Winston informed them, "but it's misplaced. The famous Egbert family digestive system is once again in fully functioning condition."

"That means he'll eat anything," Denise said. "I should know. I've seen him do it."

"And is that the famous Egbert family fishing hat?" Isabella asked. "It looks like it's been around for a while."

Winston grinned and removed the battered fishing hat from his head. It was covered with rusty old flies made of colorful twine and thread. "The guy in the vintage clothing shop told me these are all hand-tied flies," he said proudly.

"Planning to fish?" Danny asked dryly.

Winston put the hat back on his head and stared balefully at Danny. "Jealous," he said succinctly.

Everybody laughed, and Tom gestured toward Winston's plate with his fork. "Kidneys, huh? Don't you have to be on a waiting list for those?"

Winston gave Tom a superior look and shook his head sadly. "Such provincial palates," he joked. Winston put another forkful of his breakfast in his mouth, chewed, and swallowed. "Mmmm, delicious. What's the matter with you people? Have you no appreciation whatsoever for the local culture and cuisine? St. Lucia was originally a British island, and kidneys are a traditional British breakfast dish."

"Thanks for telling us," Elizabeth said, wrinkling her nose.

"This edifying information was gleaned by perusing volume C of the *Encyclopaedia Britannica* during my unfortunate confinement in the infirmary when the famous Egbert digestive system suffered a slight setback."

"This island sounds pretty neat," Danny commented. "It'll be like being in England, only with better weather."

"So is everybody up for the excursion?" Elizabeth asked.

"I think everybody will want to go," Isabella assured her. "I saw Nina this morning, and she said Bryan can't wait to get his feet on dry land again."

Noah and Alex appeared, with Jessica right behind them. Soon everybody was chatting and arguing over where to go, what to do, and when to do it.

"Shopping!" Noah exclaimed scornfully. "Who wants to go shopping?"

"I do," Isabella and Jessica said, both at the same time.

"We do too," said two more voices in unison. Elizabeth smothered a laugh when Lila and Bruce sat down with their plates.

They wore matching white silk boating shirts with their initials embroidered in blue on the pockets. Bruce wore a pair of loose silk navy slacks, and Lila had on a bright red sarong skirt.

"Great shirts," Winston said approvingly.

"We got them last night in the gift shop on the Lido deck," Bruce explained.

"I knew the minute I said the word *shopping* that Lila would turn up." Isabella laughed.

"Shopping is a girl thing," Tom said. "I

don't want to shop. I want to sightsee."

"*Some* women prefer sight-seeing," Elizabeth informed him.

"And some *men* would rather shop," Bruce said huffily.

Lila and Jessica jumped into the conversation, eagerly discussing what luxury items could be bought duty free on the island.

Elizabeth saw Noah's head swivel from side to side as they debated whether to buy Baccarat or Lalique, the two kinds of fine crystal that the islands were famous for selling at low prices.

"Eating!" Winston said, raising his voice to be heard over the shopping debate. "Now, that's what I want to do. It's food that gives you a sense of a place. Not perfume and crystal. Besides, you can buy that stuff anywhere in the United States."

"That's not the point," Isabella said, leaning past Noah to speak to Winston. "And besides, you can eat anything you want in the United States too."

"Is Winston talking about food?" Bruce asked. He turned to Winston. "Are you talking about food? Because if you want good food, there's a restaurant on this island that—"

"Hold it! Hold it!" Elizabeth cried, clapping her hands to get everybody's attention.

The noise died down, and Elizabeth smiled happily. When she had opened her eyes this morning, she'd wondered if this whole voyage was ill-fated. After Jessica's mishap, Winston's illness, Bryan's misfortunes, and her misunderstanding with Tom, she had thought this cruise had been the worst idea she'd ever had.

But now everything was different. This was what she had pictured when she planned the trip. After the William White nightmare, she wanted everyone to share a fun experience.

"We don't all have to do the same thing," she said. "Once we get to the island, I think our policy should be if it feels good, do it. Don't worry about sticking with the group. If you want to go into a shop, go. If you want to go into a restaurant, go. If we get separated, it's no problem. We'll just meet back on the ship."

"I think that's a good idea." Tom nodded. "That way everybody gets to do exactly what he or she wants."

"But I don't want to go snorkeling," Bryan argued, standing on the edge of the water.

"Bryan!" Nina groaned. "Look at that area over there. Where the little kids are. It's not even three feet deep. All you have to do is hold the mask over your face and bend over. Don't you have any curiosity about what's under the water?"

"None," Bryan said curtly.

Nina sighed unhappily and tugged at the bottom

of her bathing suit. Bryan had been silent over breakfast. During the ride from the ship to the island, his behavior had bordered on rude. And he had been surly to Winston and Denise when they'd arrived.

Nina rinsed off her mask and waded back up to the beach, where Bryan stood in his bathing suit, holding their beach bag.

He'd had a rough time, and she really needed to try to be more sympathetic. But it was hard to feel sorry for somebody who obviously felt so sorry for himself. "OK. If you don't want to snorkel, what would you like to do?" she asked sweetly.

He frowned. "Whatever you want to do," he answered.

"But everything I've suggested, you said you don't want to do," she said, forcing her voice to sound calm and logical.

"That's because everything you've suggested is either something I can't do, can't eat, or can't afford."

Nina stamped her foot. "What can't you afford?" she demanded, finally losing patience.

"I can't afford a two-thousand-dollar chandelier," he snapped. "The one you had such a fit over in that shop window."

"I didn't say let's *buy* it!" she shouted. "I said let's go in and *look* at it. Haven't you ever heard of window shopping?"

"Black men do not window-shop," he said curtly.

"Why not?" she demanded.

"Because people get nervous when they see black men peering in their shop windows. It's part of the inherent racism of the—"

"The people who live here are *black*!" she yelled in frustration.

He glowered back.

A couple of children paused in their swimming and gave them a curious look. Nina lowered her voice. "Bryan. You're just trying to be difficult."

"I am not."

"You are too."

"Why shouldn't I be difficult?" he countered. "I've been pushed off a pier, whacked on the head, barfed on, and laughed at. All things considered, it's not exactly Disneyland, is it?"

Suddenly Nina felt terrible. Poor Bryan. He really was having a horrible time. Surely there was something on the island that he would enjoy. Something that would occupy him while she parasailed.

Her eyes lingered longingly on the pontoon dock that floated almost a mile offshore. Every few minutes she heard the roar of a motorboat; it was followed by the sight of a brightly colored sail lifting someone into the blue sky.

She couldn't pass up the opportunity to parasail

in this setting. The aerial view of the island was probably spectacular. She'd remember the experience for the rest of her life.

She turned her eyes back toward the land and smiled. "I think I've discovered the answer to our problems," she said. "Look! The island cultural center is just over there. I'll parasail; you hang out in the cultural center." She gave his shoulder a shove. "Go on. You know you love that kind of thing."

Bryan nodded and walked moodily away. Nina noted with a pang of guilt that she felt as if a big cloud had lifted from her horizon. Then she dove into the water and began swimming toward the parasailing dock.

Chapter
Seventeen

"You guys go ahead," Tom said to Elizabeth and Jessica. "I'll catch up in a couple of minutes." He stopped in the doorway of The Fisherman and peered inside the shop.

"We'll go in with you," Elizabeth offered.

"No, we won't," Jessica said. "I don't want to look at fishing equipment. I want to look at jewelry and perfume."

Elizabeth's eyes met Tom's and he gave her a smile. "Go ahead," he said in a reassuring tone.

"You're sure?"

"Sure, I'm sure. Go on."

Tom stepped inside the store and let out a low whistle. It was huge. He'd never seen so much equipment in his life. He wandered over toward a counter where several fancy rods were laid out.

There was one in particular that caught his eye.

He liked the way the handle looked. It was carved wood, and his palm itched to hold it. He could almost feel the play of the line.

He reached forward and put his hand on it just as another hand reached out to touch the handle. Tom looked up in confusion. He blushed when he saw Nicole staring at him, pink with confusion herself. "Tom!"

"Nicole!"

Her eyes dropped to the counter, and he suddenly realized that his hand had folded over hers on the handle of the fishing rod. Her hand felt soft and delicate beneath his. Embarrassed, he let go and shoved his own hand into his pocket. "I didn't know you were a fishing fan," he said, casting about for something to say.

"I didn't know you were," she said.

They continued to stare at each other. Nicole tore her eyes away first. "Incredible store, isn't it?"

He shot a look around and smiled. "It's incredible, all right. I've never seen anything like it."

Her eyes flickered about and then rested curiously on his face. "Where's Elizabeth? And Jessica?"

"They're . . . uh . . . somewhere," he said lamely. "I guess I should be trying to catch up with them."

"OK," she said, smiling faintly. "See you."

There was something slightly forlorn about

her, and Tom couldn't help taking a step forward. "Are you by yourself?" he asked gently.

Nicole smiled tightly. "I might as well be."

There was a loud explosion of male laughter in the back and Tom saw Jason and Danny appear. "Tom!" Jason cried. "Glad you're here. There's a bar in the back. Let's get something to drink."

Isabella appeared from behind a counter and threaded her arm through Danny's.

"Let me get the drinks," Tom said quickly, determined to get himself out of the way. "What does everybody want?"

"Isabella?" Danny asked.

"A frozen lime drink," she answered.

"Make that two," Danny said.

"That sounds good," Jason said. "I'll have the same." He turned away to admire a handwoven creel.

Tom noticed that Jason didn't ask Nicole what she wanted. "You still drink mineral water with lemon and no ice?" he asked her with a grin. "Or would you rather have a frozen lime drink?"

Nicole's eyes widened slightly, and he knew immediately that he'd made a blunder.

Jason jerked up his head and fixed Tom with a curious smile. "How do you know what Nicole likes to drink?"

Tom noticed Isabella's eyes boring into his, and his mind went absolutely blank. "I . . ."

"We were just talking about getting something to drink when you came over," Nicole said quickly, her eyes on her shoes.

Tom wondered if Jason noticed that the tips of Nicole's ears were crimson. But Jason's attention had already been diverted by a large stuffed marlin on the back wall. "Danny," he said. "Come take a look at this. Mr. Stevens, our old biology teacher, used to have one just like it in his garage."

Nicole's eyes darted up, met Tom's, and then dropped to her shoes again. As Tom turned toward the direction of the bar, he noticed Isabella giving him a speculative stare.

"Maybe if we got a list of the ship's passengers, we could get a list of the cabin numbers assigned to SVU students. And then we could start cross-checking the names and . . ."

"We?" Elizabeth repeated. "Thanks, but no thanks. I'm not up to playing detective today."

"But Elizabeth!" Jessica protested. "Don't you want to know who saved your very own sister's life?"

Elizabeth laughed. "Maybe it's better not to know. Maybe he's like Superman or something. Once his identity is revealed, he'll lose his power."

"It really is kind of supernatural, isn't it? He's saved me, what . . . three times?"

"Let's see," Elizabeth mused. "I'm pretty convinced that it was your guardian angel who punched James Montgomery the night he tried to assault you."

"Me too," Jessica agreed. She shivered at the memory of James, drunk and hurtling in their direction like an enraged bull.

It had been dark that night on the mountaintop. Someone had stepped out of the shadows and knocked out James, giving Jessica and Elizabeth time to get into their Jeep and drive away. "And it was my guardian angel who let me out of the closet down in the parking garage of Marsden Hall when William White locked me up," Jessica said.

"OK. That's twice," Elizabeth answered.

"So pulling me out of the water was rescue number three. Elizabeth! Some guy has saved me three times. I have to know who it is! I have to know who's watching out for me." Jessica's sandals tapped against the cobblestoned streets. "I'm going to keep my eyes open every minute."

"Keep your eyes open for Tom while you're at it," Elizabeth said. "We lost him at that fishing store thirty minutes ago."

"He'll be in there for hours," Jessica predicted. "It's the largest one in the Caribbean. Let's keep going and try to find where the big perfume shop is." They turned a corner, and Jessica whistled. "Wow! Look at this."

The two girls gazed admiringly at the row of

shops that ran along the charming, tree-lined street. There were a lot of tourists streaming up and down the sidewalks, moving in and out of the shops.

Jessica's eyes searched above the crowd for a dark head and a pair of broad shoulders. Unfortunately, no one in her line of sight was tall enough to be her guardian angel.

While Elizabeth unfolded her tourist map and studied the maze of little streets, Jessica turned and stared hard to see if someone was following behind them.

The sun shone right in her eyes, blinding her. She lifted her hand to shield them and gasped as a silhouette appeared. A silhouette that stood tall, broad shouldered, and dark against the backlighting of the sun.

He walked toward her, striding purposefully up the street. Jessica's heart began to beat like a drum and her lips trembled. Suddenly he was right in front of her. With an involuntary cry of happiness, Jessica closed her eyes and threw herself forward into his arms. "It's you!" she cried. "It's you! I knew you'd come."

A pair of strong arms closed around her just in time to keep her from falling forward on the cobblestones. "Gee, it's nice to see you too, Jess. But let's not get carried away."

Jessica opened her eyes and blinked. "Tom!" She groaned in disappointment.

"Who were you expecting? Elvis?"

"I was expecting an angel."

"Huh?"

A cool ocean breeze blew up the street. Jessica's full cotton skirt whipped around her ankles and her long, loose hair flew across her eyes. "Never mind," she muttered, raking her hair back and smoothing her dress.

"Jessica's got a secret admirer," Elizabeth explained. "We think it may be her guardian angel."

"Oh?" Tom's dark eyes grew large with interest. "I didn't know you had a secret admirer," he said in a solemn tone. "A secret admirer with celestial connections sounds like a pretty good thing to have. I'd try to hang on to him if I were you."

"Ha ha!" Jessica said sourly. "I guess you think nobody admires me but jerks and losers."

"Hey!" Tom said, holding up his hands in surrender. "I was just teasing you. Don't you think you're being a little sensitive?"

"Don't you think you're being a little *insensitive*?" she countered.

"Break it up, you two," Elizabeth interrupted. "Things are going well, and everybody's having a good time. So play nice—don't fight."

Tom caught the warning look in Elizabeth's eyes and bit back his next retort. He was really starting to sympathize with Nicole's concern that

191

Jason preferred his guy friends over her. Sometimes—like now—Tom felt as if Elizabeth was just dating him because she for some reason thought it was her duty to humor him. Obviously, it was Jessica's company that she really valued.

Tom had stayed in the fishing store just long enough to be polite. Then he'd excused himself. He'd tried to hint to Danny once or twice that Jason and Nicole could use some time to themselves, but the usually perceptive Danny had been completely dense.

Nicole was clearly unhappy about the way her wedding cruise was turning out. Tom wasn't too happy about the way things were going either, but he was trying to be a good sport. He really did feel for Jessica—he didn't want her to be lonely. But running into Nicole kept knocking him off balance.

In spite of their determination to have as little contact as possible, the sparks between them were flying, and the only way he knew to put them out was a big splash of Elizabeth. Tom sighed, wishing he could explain the situation to his girlfriend.

"Where is everybody?" he asked. "I haven't seen a familiar face since I left the fishing store."

"Winston and Denise went to the cultural center. Lila and Bruce are pricing Lalique. Noah and Alex went to the bird sanctuary, and we haven't seen Nina or Bryan since we got here."

"There's a bird sanctuary?"

Elizabeth nodded and placed her finger on the map. "Right around there, I think."

"Wow. I'd like to see that." He took the map from her and studied it, rubbing his neck. "Looks like I get the bus a couple of blocks away. Who wants to go to the bird sanctuary?"

"I want to look for perfume," Jessica announced.

With great difficulty, Tom refrained from rolling his eyes.

Elizabeth seemed to sense his irritation and stepped closer to him. "Jessica's in a pretty good mood," she said in a low tone. "I'll help her find the perfume store and you go to the sanctuary. Then I'll let Jess go explore on her own and meet you for a snack at the Beach Café at three. We can take a walk by the water before going back to the ship. Just you and me."

He smiled, and the tight, uneasy feeling around his heart began to relax. If he and Elizabeth could just spend a little time alone, he'd get his bearings again. "Sounds good to me."

Elizabeth kissed him lightly on the lips. "See you at three."

"Come on, Liz!" Jessica called impatiently. "Let's find the perfume shop." If her secret admirer did reveal himself, Jessica was determined to smell good.

In a moment Elizabeth was leading the way again, tracing the route on the map and navigating the complicated streets and lanes that led to the central business district of the island.

They made several turns, making their way through streets thick with tourists from the various cruise ships that were anchored just off St. Lucia.

The crowd grew bigger as they neared the central shopping district, and suddenly Jessica felt the hair on the back of her neck rise. *Somebody's watching us—me!*

She whirled and scanned the street. There were several tall, dark young men. Was one of them staring at her?

Elizabeth was several yards ahead, and Jessica hurried to catch up, turning to look behind her every few steps.

They turned onto a quiet and deserted side street. "This doesn't look right," Elizabeth muttered, coming to a stop and looking down at the wilted map.

Jessica's eyes darted to the pavement as a shadow fell across the sidewalk. Someone stood just around the corner of the building—someone tall.

With her heart in her throat, she began to walk toward the corner. She would have to take him by surprise. Obviously he was too shy to ever approach her on his own.

Jessica paused at the corner of the building, preparing to spring. As she dove around the corner, another breeze roared down the block and blew her hair across her eyes, blinding her. She clutched at his shirt. "Don't run away," she commanded. "I think I'm in love with you."

The figure rocked backward and screamed. "Hey, hey, hey, young lady! Cut that out!"

Jessica released her grasp, pushed back her hair, and shrieked. "Oh, no!"

A very tall old man in a loud Hawaiian shirt and double-knit pants was nervously checking his wrist and patting his back pocket, making sure his wallet and watch were still in place. He fixed Jessica with a suspicious glare. "Right. Everything present and accounted for. Nobody pickpockets C. J. Kravitz from Yonkers! I didn't just fall off the turnip truck, you know. This is my fifth cruise."

"I'm not a pickpocket," Jessica began.

Elizabeth came around the corner. "Jess? What's going on?"

C. J. Kravitz from Yonkers put a hand to his forehead. "Great! Twin pickpockets. *Police!*" he shouted.

Jessica grabbed Elizabeth's arm and pulled. "Let's get out of here!"

Jessica's sandals weren't made for running, especially on cobblestones. As they thundered down the street, she wished she'd taken Elizabeth's advice and worn sneakers.

"I should have known that somehow, you'd get me into trouble," Elizabeth panted angrily, running beside her.

"We're not in trouble," Jessica puffed.

"Then why are we running?"

"Habit," Jessica answered, lowering her head and running even faster.

"Hey, Nicole. Look at these. They'd be beautiful with our china," Jason said.

Isabella put down the goblet she was admiring and followed Nicole over to where Jason stood beside a set of crystal decanters. "Look at the enamel on the stoppers. It's the same color as the border on our dinner plates."

"You're right," Nicole answered. Her voice was devoid of enthusiasm, just as it had been all day.

"Would you like them for a wedding present?" Jason asked. "My parents told me to use their credit card to buy ourselves something."

Nicole shrugged. "I guess."

"Come on," Danny whispered to Isabella. "Let's walk over there and let them talk about it by themselves." He gently propelled her into an adjoining room that glittered with crystal.

"Doesn't Nicole seem a little unhappy?" Isabella asked.

"Nah. She was probably just feeling inhibited because we were standing there. People like privacy when they're making decisions about spending money." Danny gazed around the expensive shop. "Wow! Look at that vase."

"But she's been like that all morning," Isabella pressed. "Didn't you notice when she . . ."

But Danny didn't let her finish. His eyes suddenly grew wide, and he started striding toward the glass door that faced the street. After a few more steps he was in the road, where several tourists were preparing to board a charter bus.

"Danny?" Isabella cried, running out of the shop behind him. "What are you . . ." She broke off as Danny leaned forward and grabbed a large, tough-looking teenager by the lapels of his leather jacket.

"Give it back," Danny ordered the boy.

"I don't know what you're talking about," the guy sneered.

"I'm talking about the wallet you just slipped out of that lady's purse," Danny answered.

Several women standing on the street automatically checked their purses. At least four of them gasped.

"My wallet's gone!" someone cried.

"So is mine!" an elderly man exclaimed.

"Oh, Harold!" his wife moaned.

"My wallet is gone too," a young woman with a baby wailed.

Danny released the lapels of the guy's jacket. "Give them back," he ordered.

The boy took a few steps backward and lifted his shoulders, loosening the fit of the oversize bomber jacket.

Isabella pressed her hands to her mouth, sick with fear. Big jackets usually hid guns. Was Danny crazy?

"How many times do I have to say it?" Danny demanded. "Give them back. Now!"

The boy stared at Danny, seeming to deliberate as his hand reached slowly toward the breast of his jacket. He flung it open with a violent jerk, and Isabella screamed and covered her ears.

But there was no sound of a gun going off.

Instead, she heard the gentle plopping of leather wallets as they fell to the pavement from the lining of the jacket.

The police appeared from out of nowhere, and the next thing Isabella knew, one pair of policemen was leading the boy away while another pair shook Danny's hand, congratulating him. A fifth policeman sorted through the wallets, returning them to their owners.

Isabella hurried to Danny's side.

". . . where you have tourists, you have thieves," the policeman was saying. "And thieves make tourists stay home. Thank you for your help. You're a very brave man."

"He's a very *stupid* man," Isabella protested angrily.

Danny and the policeman both looked at her

with astonished expressions. "That guy could have had a gun," she choked. "He might have killed you. And for what? For nothing, that's what. Danny, don't ever do that again."

Danny frowned and lifted his shoulders in a bewildered shrug. "How could I do anything else? To witness a crime and do nothing is as bad as being a criminal yourself. It's not ethical."

Before Isabella could respond, Jason and Nicole came running out of the store. "Unbelievable!" Jason said. "But totally unsurprising." He squeezed Danny's shoulder. "He's always been like that," he said. "When we were kids, it was Danny who chased away the bullies."

"Jason," Nicole whispered in a faint voice. "I think I'd like to go back to the ship."

"Sure," Jason said over his shoulder. "You go on. Don't worry about me."

In spite of the horror of the moment, Isabella had to smother a laugh. Obviously Nicole *wasn't* worrying about him. She was expecting *him* to worry about *her*. And Jason wasn't.

"Hey! What's going on?" a familiar baritone asked.

Tom Watts came striding around the corner, a backpack slung over his shoulder. Isabella noted that his smile immediately disappeared when his eyes rested on Nicole. They bounced off her face and cut quickly away toward Danny.

"Danny just faced down some punk kid pick-pocket single-handedly," Jason said proudly. "He made him hand over all the wallets he took."

An elderly couple stood politely to the side, apparently wanting to speak to Danny.

"Yes, ma'am?" Danny said in his customary soft, good-natured voice.

"I just wanted to thank you," the woman said.

"My wife and I saved for three years to come on this trip," the old man said. "It's our fiftieth wedding anniversary, and I had all the money for the trip in my wallet. Cash money!" He shook his head. "If that boy had gotten our wallets, I don't know what we would have done."

"I *told* you to get traveler's checks," his wife said tartly. It was obvious from her loving but impatient tone that this had been the subject of a long-standing dispute.

"Traveler's checks!" he said with a derisive snort. "Newfangled nonsense. Cash. That's the way to go. I believe in paying cash—all the way."

"Traveler's checks are just like cash," Danny said politely. "And they're replaceable if lost or stolen."

The man waved his hand and snorted again. "Ha! Traveler's checks!"

"You might as well talk to a wall," the woman said indulgently. "But we sure do thank you."

The man beamed at Danny. "I never saw anything like it. What a brave young man."

They walked away, and everybody laughed.

"Since when are traveler's checks newfangled?" Jason asked. "Weren't they invented several decades ago?"

Isabella couldn't believe that no one else was concerned about Danny's safety. "Danny, it's stupid to risk your life to protect money. You tell him, Tom." She turned to Tom, expecting his support. But Tom was staring at Nicole, who was staring fixedly over the horizon. "Tom?" Isabella pressed.

Tom jumped and his face flushed a deep red. "Sorry. What did you say?"

"Isabella," Danny said, "let's go talk."

Isabella let Danny walk her a few yards away. "Izzy," he said softly. "You're right. It's stupid to risk your life to protect money. But it wasn't just money to those old people. That money represented three years of saving for something special that they could share. And I don't think it's ethical for any citizen to stand by and let some lowlife deprive two nice old people of what's rightfully theirs. Ordinary citizens have an obligation to intervene where they think they can."

Over Danny's shoulder, Isabella watched Nicole say something to Jason. "Sure, go ahead," she heard Jason say to his fiancée.

Nicole said something that Isabella couldn't quite catch.

"But I don't want to go back to the boat," Jason said. He grabbed Tom's arm. "Tom, do me a big favor, will you? Walk Nicole back to the pier and see that she gets on the tender? I'd really appreciate it."

The tender was the small shuttle boat that ferried passengers back and forth from the island pier to the ship.

Tom looked momentarily horrified.

"Don't you want to go with me?" Nicole asked Jason in a small voice. "It would give us some time together."

"We've got the rest of our lives to be together," Jason said, giving her a big hug. "I've only got a few days to hang with my old buddy."

It took all of Isabella's self-control not to groan out loud. Sometimes when guys got together, they were unbelievably stupid.

Danny was still droning on and on about ethics and his obligation as a world citizen. "Danny," Isabella interrupted suddenly.

"Hmm?"

"Do you think there's something going on between Tom and Nicole?"

Danny's eyes grew large. Then he blinked and shook his head. "Say that again."

"I know this is a totally different subject, but

do you think there's something going on between Tom and Nicole?"

"What would make you think something like that?"

"I'm just picking up on vibes. Signals. It's like there's something going on between the two of them and—"

"Isabella, sometimes you are so off base." Danny ran his hand over his short hair and grinned. "Nicole and Tom? No way. I mean, Nicole and Jason are engaged. Tom is in love with Elizabeth. And everybody's hardly been on the ship a day. When would they have had time to fall for each other?"

Isabella watched Tom and Nicole disappear down the dusty road that led to the pier. Then she squinted up at Danny's open and trusting face and smiled. He was a rare personality. Until Danny saw a person do something with his own eyes—as in the case of the pickpocket—he would never think badly of anyone.

Isabella ruefully concluded that she would do well to take a lesson from Danny. All the points he had raised were absolutely valid. Her suspicions were absurd. They said more about the flaws in her own character than anything else. Obviously she wasn't as trusting a person as she thought she was.

"You're right," Isabella said softly. She took his

hand, determined to say nothing more about his altercation with the pickpocket. The same qualities that attracted her to Danny were the qualities that had led him to confront the thief. So why was she trying to change him?

And her suspicions about Tom and Nicole were groundless. Still . . . Tom and Nicole's behavior when they were together was definitely odd.

Chapter Eighteen

Bryan stared glumly at the photographs that lined the wall of the Coral Reef Gallery. There were enough glossy color photos of undersea life to line the walls of four rooms.

It had been an interesting exhibit—the first three times he'd gone around it. Wasn't Nina *ever* going to get enough parasailing?

"Hey, Bryan!"

He turned and saw Denise giving him a big smile and a wave. He smiled back. Other than the fact that she was Winston Egbert's girlfriend, he didn't have anything against her. In fact, he liked her a lot.

She hurried over to him. "Great exhibit, huh? Where's Nina?"

"She's parasailing," Bryan explained.

"How come you're not doing it with her?"

"I, uh . . ." The last thing in the world Bryan wanted to admit was that he was afraid to parasail and that he couldn't even swim. He'd looked ridiculous enough over the past twenty-four hours. "It's just not my thing," he said quickly.

"Mine either," Denise said. "Come outside to the café and have some lemonade with Winston and me. Our treat."

Bryan paused.

"Please," she said sweetly. "Winston feels awful about . . . well . . . you know. . . ."

Bryan felt too embarrassed to even answer. He didn't want to have lemonade with Winston. But he didn't know how to refuse without looking childish.

He wished Denise had never run into him.

"Come on," she urged. "Let's try to be friends, OK?"

Bryan took a deep breath and nodded, steeling himself to meet face-to-face with Winston. The deep breaths were a good idea. They had a calming effect and took the edge off his irritation.

Bryan took another couple of big gulps as they stepped outside into the balmy air. The sunlight sparkled on the surface of the ocean, and when he gazed up, he felt his heart swell until he thought it might burst.

Strong and shapely, Nina soared above him on the bright yellow-and-red wings of the parasail.

She was like some nimble, beautiful Caribbean butterfly. A goddess right out of a folktale.

For Nina, he would do anything. He'd even make peace with a menace called Winston Egbert. He would smile and laugh and have a good time. He would lie facedown in the water if she wanted him to. A great sense of shame washed over him. A real man would be doing everything he could to make her happy and not worry about his own dignity.

"We've got a table over there," Denise said, pointing toward a café area set up beside the gallery, overlooking the sea. Winston lifted a hand and waved.

As of now, Bryan resolved, he was turning over a new leaf. Nobody on ship would be more affable and easygoing than Bryan Nelson. Bryan curved his lips into a smile. From now on, he was going to be Mr. Charm—he'd be the schmooze king of the *Homecoming Queen*. "Winston," he said cheerfully. "Nice to see you."

Winston beamed back, clearly surprised to be getting such a warm greeting. "Sit down, sit down," he invited, gesturing toward a chair while beckoning eagerly to a waiter.

"Thank you," Bryan said in his most cordial voice. "I'd love to."

Winston adjusted the chair and Bryan sat. "Ouch!" Bryan screamed as a series of sharp, piercing pains assaulted his backside. "What the . . ." He leapt up and turned to see what had punctured his behind. Then he heard Winston moan, "Ohhhh, noooooo!"

Bryan had sat down right on top of Winston's vintage fishing hat. Bryan carefully detached the hat while gritting his teeth against the pain. "I think this is yours," he said to Winston, letting the hat dangle from his fingertips as if it were a dirty diaper.

Winston sank into his chair and covered his face with his hands. "I forgot it was on the chair. I'm sorry. I'm really, really sorry."

"Bryan," Denise said in a worried tone. "Those are old hooks. When was the last time you had a tetanus shot?"

"I don't know," Bryan said, as calmly as he could manage. "Would you excuse me, please? I think I'd better go find the doctor."

Winston smiled. "Oh. Well. At least I can help you there." He pointed toward the parasailing dock, where Nina was being helped from the water by a tall, well-built man in a skintight bathing suit. "That's Dr. Daniels out there."

"I'm sorry," Bruce said helplessly. "Maybe I'm an insensitive jerk, but I just don't see why you have to burst into tears every time we look at a piece of Lalique." He pulled a monogrammed leather tissue holder from his windbreaker and handed Lila a Kleenex.

She dabbed at the corners of her streaming eyes. "Tisiano's family had one of the largest collections of Lalique in Italy." Lila sniffed. "Every time I see a piece, I think about him and . . ." She broke off and burst into fresh sobs.

"OK. I can see that," Bruce said. "But if looking at crystal is going to get you all upset, why did you suggest we go look at Lalique?"

"I don't know," Lila choked out. When she'd suggested it, she hadn't even thought about the connection of Lalique to Tisiano. It was only when they began to wander from store to store, admiring the beautiful birds and objets d'art, that she realized how closely the two were related in her mind.

She remembered the birds that had adorned the mantel in the library. And the iridescent vase in the sitting room that had so beautifully reflected the afternoon Italian sun.

How could she have forgotten? When Bruce had asked her what she wanted to see, the word *Lalique* had sprung almost automatically to her lips. It was as if she had been almost *compelled* to suggest they look at something that would remind her of Tisiano. It was as if someone had whispered the word in her ear, and she had simply repeated it without thinking.

"We could have looked at clothes," Bruce continued. "We could have shopped for jewelry, or—"

"Is our entire relationship based on *things*?" Lila demanded, swallowing her sobs and staring at Bruce's handsome face.

Bruce replaced his leather tissue holder and put his hands on his hips. "I told you before, Lila. I'm not going to apologize for who I am. Or what I am. Or the way I live. I'm a material guy. That doesn't mean I only care about *things*," he said, imitating the scornful tone Lila had used. "But *things* are what make the world go round. Making things. Buying things. If people stopped making things and buying things, the world would stop spinning. Quit beating up on me. And quit beating up on yourself."

He took her arm and began walking her back down the street of quaint shops. One or two shopkeepers smiled and waved at them from their doorways. "You think these people are smiling at us because they're glad to see us coming? Because they enjoy our company? I don't think so. They're glad to see us coming because we'll buy some of their *things*. Consumerism is a form of diplomacy."

Tisiano would have hated Bruce, Lila thought unhappily. He would have regarded him as crass. She had often felt gauche and awkward when she was with Tisiano.

Tisiano had had generations of wealth behind him. He'd had generations of training in the art of being graciously rich. He never paraded his wealth. He lived well, and he enjoyed beautiful objects. But it was all done in a low-key, unobtrusive fashion.

Furthermore, he had chosen to work hard. He'd devoted himself to the family business rather than living the life of a free-spending playboy. The result was that he had never had as much time for Lila as she would have liked.

Bruce's voice droned on and on, extolling the upside of being rich. He was expressing all the feelings that Lila had about money but had been afraid to voice in front of Tisiano for fear of offending his sensibility.

It was nice to hear somebody speak his mind. And it was nice to hear somebody say things bluntly, without worrying about what people thought.

With a flash of insight, Lila realized that Bruce Patman was much more right for her than Tisiano had been. She and Bruce were cut from the same mold. Now she felt even more mixed up. Did that mean the deep love she had felt for Tisiano had been wrong? Had she been mistaken?

Did her compatibility with Bruce Patman somehow cancel out the feelings she had for Tisiano? Feelings that seemed to increasingly lose their sharp edges.

It was hurting less and less to think about him.

"Lila!" Bruce said gently. "Are you listening to me?"

"I'm listening," Lila said, letting the ocean breeze dry the tears on her cheeks.

"No way," Gin-Yung argued, blowing a large bubble and then popping it with a loud snap. "Miles Drury never had anything like that kind of a batting average." She shrugged on a blue blazer as a chilly ocean breeze blew past, ruffling her short, blunt-cut bob.

It was funny, Todd thought, how neat and petite she looked—even in rumpled, loose-fitting khakis, a man's oxford cloth shirt with the shirttail out, and penny loafers. It seemed to be her uniform. He'd never seen her in anything else.

"He did too," Todd insisted, defending a baseball player who had excelled for years in the minors but had died in obscurity before making it to the majors.

Gin-Yung came to a stop and put her hands on her hips. "Ten bucks says you're wrong."

Todd flung out his hands. "Oh, no. Where I come from, a gentleman doesn't take ten bucks off a lady."

Gin-Yung laughed. "Ten bucks says you're wrong," she repeated. "And where I come from, it's no sin to take ten bucks off a sucker."

"You're on," Todd said. "But how are we going to settle this?"

Gin-Yung blew another bubble and then reached into her back pocket and held up a small, thin, paperback book.

"A calorie counter?" Todd guessed, remembering seeing Elizabeth refer to one almost constantly during her dieting days.

"You wish," Gin-Yung said. "It's the pocket stat guide. Everything you want to know about baseball statistics in print so small it'll give you a migraine. All sportswriters have them." She flipped through the little reference book, squinted at a page, and handed the book to him. "Read it and weep."

Todd felt a wide smile spread across his face. He'd never felt so happy about being wrong. Gin-Yung was a walking sports encyclopedia. He'd never ever met a girl who knew more about sports than he did.

It was unnerving. But very exhilarating.

He handed the book back to her and reached down into his pocket. With a deft motion, he fished up a ten-dollar bill, held it up so she could see the denomination, then put it into her waiting hand.

"Thank you," she said with a grin. "Wanna play pool sometime? I don't know too much about it, but—"

213

"Oh, knock it off," Todd answered quickly. "I'll bet you could beat every guy on the ship."

"Probably," she answered. "Come on. I'll buy you a soda."

Side by side, they ambled down a cobblestone street. She walked like a guy—with her hands shoved down deep into her front pockets.

"This is nice," he said after they had talked sports for three blocks.

"What's nice?"

"Being able to talk to a girl like she was a guy."

Gin-Yung stopped and gave him a quizzical smile. "Is this the let's-be-friends speech?"

Todd's mouth fell open. "No," he protested. "I mean, yes. I mean . . . no. I mean, *yes*, I do want to be your friend. But no, I don't want to *just* be your friend—unless, of course, that's what you want. And if that's what you want, then I . . ."

Her eyes twinkled, and it was obvious she was trying hard not to smile at his discomfort.

Todd smiled uneasily, worried that in spite of her smile, he was about to offend her. "I really didn't mean anything by that remark other than that I'm having a great time with you. I'm enjoying your company. And as far as being friends—or being more than friends . . ." He took a deep breath and shrugged. "I hadn't thought about it," he said.

She took a step forward, lifted her face, and kissed him softly. "Think about it now," she said.

214

*　　*　　*

At a quarter to four that afternoon, Tom finally pulled some money from his pocket to pay for his coffee; he left the little café and its romantic view of the ocean.

Apparently Elizabeth wasn't going to show up. Tom sighed, wishing he'd stuck with Elizabeth and Jessica instead of wandering off on his own and running into Nicole again.

It seemed like the harder he tried to avoid her, the more he bumped into her. And everybody seemed determined to push them together.

He couldn't believe Jason. If Nicole had been Tom's girlfriend, he would have walked her to the tender himself. Obviously Jason trusted her. And trusted Tom.

It was nice to be trusted, but at what point did "being trusted" become "being taken for granted"?

Jason is a lucky guy, Tom had said to Nicole when he walked her away from the scene outside the crystal shop. *I'm not sure he realizes quite how lucky he is.*

I don't think Elizabeth realizes how lucky she is either, Nicole had answered. *If she did, you wouldn't be available to walk me to the tender.*

Tom hadn't known what to say to that remark, and the two of them had walked to the pier and waited for the little boat in awkward silence. He'd breathed a sigh of relief when she had gotten safely onto the boat and headed back to the ship. Then he'd headed for the Beach Café to wait for Elizabeth.

But she hadn't come.

Why?

He still felt oddly guilty after last night. He'd come closer than he liked to admit to kissing Nicole. And he felt like it was written all over his face. Had Elizabeth somehow found out about him and Nicole? Was that why she hadn't turned up to meet him?

Get a grip, Watts, he ordered himself. Elizabeth and Jessica had probably gotten so busy doing something together that they lost track of time. Jessica probably had some new kind of crisis.

He wished Jessica's secret admirer would come out into the open. As long as Jessica was unattached, she was always going to be around. And whenever Jessica was around, there was trouble. And whenever there was trouble with Jessica, Elizabeth jumped in to straighten it out. As a result, Jessica was a permanent third wheel.

Or more accurately, Tom was a permanent third wheel. Did Elizabeth have any idea how left out he felt?

If Jessica's secret admirer didn't turn up by tonight, Tom decided to play matchmaker himself. There were a lot of good-looking guys onboard.

Guys without girlfriends. Surely he could get one of them interested in a beautiful blonde like Jessica.

Then he could devote himself to establishing warmer relations with Elizabeth—assuming Jessica didn't wind up going overboard again.

Tom checked his watch and quickened his step. The next tender would be leaving in just a few minutes.

"Hey, Tom! Wait up!"

Tom turned and saw Nina running up the street behind him with the ship's doctor.

"Have you seen Elizabeth and Jessica?" Tom asked Nina.

"Yeah," she answered. "I saw them on the last boat."

"The last boat? You mean they left the island already?" Tom scratched his head in confusion.

"I saw Danny, Jason, and Isabella on the last boat too. I think this is the last tender," she said.

"You're right," the doctor answered. "It is. So we'd better hurry."

"Are we leaving anybody behind?" Tom asked.

"I'm not sure," Nina said nervously. "Have you seen Bryan?"

Tom shook his head, and Nina gave the doctor an inquiring look. "Rich, what happens to the people who miss the boat?" she asked.

"They have a very big problem," he answered breezily. Then he laughed.

*   *   *

Nina stood on the pier, listening to Dr. Daniels describe the incredible parasailing offered in South America. He knew a lot about parasailing. He knew a lot about a lot of things. Richard Daniels had a very wide range of interests.

And he was obviously interested in Nina. It was flattering, but Nina was a little worried about the effect it might have on Bryan. On the other hand, a little jealousy might serve Bryan well. Maybe he'd realize that he needed to pay a little more attention to her.

Nina made up her mind that the minute they got back on the ship, she was going to have a serious talk with her boyfriend. It was time they sparked up some major chemistry.

She tapped her foot and looked around anxiously. Where was Bryan, anyway? She hadn't seen him since she sent him off to the cultural center. And the tender that was drawing toward the pier was the last one.

Seconds later, the boat had docked. Nina was shocked to see Bryan in it. He must have gone back to the ship earlier, and now he was coming back so that he could accompany her. "Bryan!" She smiled. "How nice."

But as soon as she got close to the tender, Nina saw Bryan stand carefully, and she noticed that he had a suitcase in his hand. Wordlessly Bryan stepped out of the boat and onto the pier.

"Bryan! What's going on?"

He gave her a long look. "I've had it with ships. I've had it with Winston Egbert. I've had it with the infirmary. And I've had it with you. I'm going home." He turned and began stalking away.

That did it. Nina dropped her beach bag on the pier and took a deep breath so she could project her voice over the sound of the sea and the screeching of the gulls. "You just go on, then!" she yelled. "Because I've had it with you, too!"

Denise banged happily on the steel drum. She'd always wanted to play with a Caribbean steel drum band and so had Winston. They had stumbled onto a very friendly group of street musicians who, after a few minutes of conversation, had invited them to join in.

It had taken a while to get the hang of the instrument. But for the past hour or so, they had really begun to catch on. She could see where this activity might get to be habit forming. Having started, she found it was hard to stop.

The beat was intoxicating. The happy, bell-like sound of the steel drums produced a kind of euphoria. Denise cast a loving look toward Winston as he happily banged away at his steel drum.

Winston might have his faults, but he was the kind of guy who made friends everywhere he went—and he always knew how to have fun. The only person who wasn't too crazy about him was Bryan Nelson.

For some reason, that relationship seemed to be cursed. Maybe it was time Winston stopped trying to befriend Bryan. Clearly a warm relationship between them just wasn't in the stars.

But a warm relationship with Winston suited Denise just fine. Being Winston's girlfriend was a nonstop adventure.

The attractive, dark-skinned singers drew out their last note and Denise and Winston banged their drums, bringing the music to a crescendo before breaking off with a dramatic flourish.

"Very nice!" the leader of the group said, taking the drumsticks from Denise and Winston. "You must come back and visit us again. You have a lot of potential."

Winston grinned. "We'd love to come back. But I guess in the meantime, we'd better get back to our ship." He looked down at his watch and the color drained from his face. "Oh, no," he whispered.

"What's wrong?" Denise asked.

Winston shook his wrist, then lifted the watch to his ear. "Oh, no," he croaked again.

"Winston. What is it?"

"My watch. It's stopped. I guess the ocean air gummed up the works."

Denise felt her heart sink into her stomach. "What are you telling me?"

"I'm telling you that the ship left thirty minutes ago."

"You mean . . ."

Winston nodded. "We're marooned!"

Chapter
Nineteen

_____

"I can't believe it," Bruce said, sinking his fork into a thick slice of four-layer chocolate cake. "It's like some kind of horror movie. Our first day out at sea, and we lose three of our party."

On the other side of the table, fresh tears began trickling down Nina's cheeks.

"Bruce!" Elizabeth snapped. "We haven't _lost_ anybody." She turned toward Nina. "Don't cry," she said, offering her a fresh napkin to wipe her tears.

"But what's going to happen to them?" Danny asked. "How do they catch up with the ship?"

"Bryan won't _want_ to catch up." Nina sniffled. "He's probably already on a plane headed back to California."

"Winston and Denise are grown-ups," Noah

said. "I'm sure they'll figure out how to find the ship at the next port of call."

"You don't know Winston," Jessica said dryly. "He couldn't find his way out of a paper bag."

"Jess!" Elizabeth said sharply. "That's not very nice."

Tom balled his fists underneath the table. On Elizabeth's left sat Jessica—whose typical antics had ruined their afternoon on the island and caused Elizabeth and Jessica to come back early to avoid the police.

Which was why Elizabeth had stood him up at the Beach Café.

On Elizabeth's right was Nina, who had spent the whole meal weeping over Bryan. Tom couldn't figure out what the problem was. Bryan clearly wasn't having any fun. He and Nina weren't getting along. She'd been flirting outrageously with the doctor ever since they got onboard. So what was she crying about? What had she expected to happen?

And why didn't Elizabeth just leave Nina alone? Why didn't Elizabeth quit mothering Nina and Jessica and monitoring everybody else's behavior? Why couldn't she just concentrate on herself? And on him?

"Jess is right," Bruce said scornfully. "Winston is a funny guy. But let's face it. He's a klutz."

Lila giggled, and Isabella glared at her and

223

Bruce. "I happen to think Winston is a very smart guy. Being funny requires a great deal of intelligence. Right, Danny?"

But Danny didn't respond. He just stared straight ahead with a glum expression on his face. Sun and food and the waves had gotten to Jason. He was in the infirmary with a bad case of seasickness, and Danny looked like a fourth grader whose best friend couldn't come out and play.

Tonight's dinner was a lot less festive than last night's. In fact, the laughter and chatter level had dropped by at least fifty percent.

The only member of their group who looked moderately happy was Todd. And he wasn't sitting with them. He was across the room with a girl Tom didn't even know.

Elizabeth glared at Bruce. "Stop sneering at everybody, would you?" She stared at Jessica. "You too. Sometimes this whole crowd is just so unpleasant to be around."

Tom dropped his fork and let it clatter on his plate. "Why don't *you* quit telling everybody what they can and can't say?"

Elizabeth's mouth opened, and she gasped, "What do you mean by that?"

"Sometimes you're such a control freak," he said. "If people want to sneer, let them sneer. If people want to argue, let them argue."

"I didn't plan this trip so that people could

waste it arguing. We're *supposed* to be having a good time," she practically spat.

"I don't see anybody having one," he responded in a caustic tone.

"Is that my fault?"

"Maybe!" Tom threw down his napkin.

The unprecedented spectacle of Tom Watts and Elizabeth Wakefield exchanging angry words seemed to stop everyone mid-sentence. A hushed, embarrassed silence descended on the table.

Elizabeth's lips trembled slightly. Then she jumped up. "Excuse me," she choked, hurrying out of the dining room.

Jessica gave Tom a reproachful look. "Good one, Tom." She put her own napkin on the table and hurried after Elizabeth.

"Wow!" Bruce said. "Bryan was pretty smart to bail while he could. This cruise is rapidly going nowhere."

Nina let out a fresh wail, stood, and ran from the dining room, weeping.

"Bruce," Lila said in a low tone, "I think maybe we should call it a night. Everything we say seems to make somebody mad."

Bruce lifted his eyebrows, took a last bite of his dessert, and then politely pulled out Lila's chair for her. "Night, guys."

Noah pushed the food around on his plate and groaned.

"What's the matter with *you*?" Tom asked, sounding more antagonistic than he meant to.

"Don't misdirect your anger at me," Noah responded tartly.

Tom's eyes widened. "Whoa! That's pretty tough talk from a shrink." The minute he heard his own words hanging in the air, he hated himself. He couldn't believe he was really acting this way. But he just couldn't help it. He was sick with disappointment over the way things were turning out.

Noah's pale, shocked face turned green. He pressed his napkin to his mouth and hurried from the table. "Noah!" Alex cried, running out of the room behind him.

"And then there were three," Isabella said softly.

"Is there something in the water?" Danny asked in a tone of disbelief. "What's going on around here?"

Tom stood. "I don't know," he muttered. "But I think I need some air."

He hurried out of the depressing dining room, practically running toward the stairs. He climbed to the upper deck as fast as he could. His frustration, anger, and confusion level were off the scale. If he didn't get some peace and quiet for a few minutes, the top of his head was going to blow off.

Fortunately there was no one on the upper deck. Tom gripped the rail and breathed in the fresh air. The moon was full, and its golden reflection stared up at Tom with a mocking smile.

A soft hand covered his. "Is Elizabeth in the infirmary too?"

Tom turned and saw Nicole's luminous eyes staring into his as if looking for some kind of answer.

"No," Tom whispered. "She's . . ." He hung his head. "She's not too happy with me right now."

"Then she's a fool."

"I think I'm the fool," Tom said hoarsely. "I lost my temper . . . *again* . . . and . . ."

Her fingertips reached up and touched his lips. "Shhhh," she said. Nicole's dark eyes grew even larger, and without warning, they were in each other's arms. Her lips pressed against his, and a wave of chills rippled up and down his spine.

"Oh, Tom," she murmured. She tightened her arms around him, and his lips traveled the length of her neck.

There were two successive gasps behind them. Startled, Tom released his hold on Nicole and she fell back against the rail. He whirled and saw Elizabeth and Danny standing not four feet away.

It was obvious that they had seen the whole

thing. "Elizabeth . . ." Tom began. "Let me explain."

But Elizabeth turned and ran, disappearing down the stairway. Tom turned toward Danny for help. But Danny looked even angrier than Elizabeth. The vein in his temple throbbed as he appeared to think very hard about something. The last thing Tom saw was Danny's huge fist speeding toward him.

"Am I right, or am I wrong?" Bruce demanded. "Is there some kind of sour karma on this boat or not?"

Lila pulled her silky sweater tighter around her and closed her eyes. They stood on the flat roof of the uppermost deck.

"It's like this ship's got some kind of curse on it. Some kind of voodoo."

"Stop it," she said quietly. "Stop it, please."

"What's the matter? What did I say?"

Lila's heart was racing and her head was throbbing. It was silly. It was nuts. But maybe Tisiano's angry spirit was walking the decks, angered at the sight of his young wife in the arms of another man. So angry, he was determined to ruin the cruise for her and everyone else. "Please don't say anything else."

"Lila!" Bruce took her arms. "I've tried to be patient. To make this trip something special for us.

You and me. Not you and me and a ghost. Can't you please, please, let go of whatever it is that's making you so unhappy?" He bent his head, and she felt his breath against her ear.

"I'm trying," she said with a shuddering breath. "I'm trying."

His hands raced up and down her arms, and his voice shook with emotion as he breathed into her neck. "Whatever it is—guilt, grief, anger—let it go. Throw it over the side right now, and let's get on with our lives."

Lila lifted her arms and wrapped them around Bruce's neck, pulling his body closer to hers. His kisses would make her forget everything else. His arms would protect her from imaginary jealous husbands. Bruce's lips were hungry, and the boat rocked beneath her feet.

Then there was a roaring sound in the sky, and a sudden and violent wind practically tore them apart.

"My God!" Bruce shouted over the noise. "It's a helicopter."

Lila clutched at her scarf to keep it from blowing away. She stared in amazement as the helicopter made an ungainly landing a few yards away. As soon as the wheels touched the flat deck, the door to the helicopter popped open and an elegant, handsome man stepped out.

Lila's heart leapt to her throat and she began

to tremble from head to toe. It was insane. It was impossible. Her eyes were playing tricks on her.

The man began striding toward her, and Lila's hands flew to her mouth. *"Tisiano!"* she screamed, before fainting into Bruce's arms.

Now that Elizabeth has caught Tom in the arms of another woman, will she seek out her old boyfriend, Todd Wilkins, for comfort? Find out in Sweet Valley University 13, SS HEARTBREAK.

We hope you enjoyed reading this book. If you would like to receive further information about available titles in the Bantam series, just write to the following address, with your name and address: Kim Prior, Bantam Books, 61–63 Uxbridge Road, Ealing, London W5 5SA.

If you live in Australia or New Zealand and would like more information about the series, please write to:

Sally Porter
Transworld Publishers
(Australia) Pty Ltd
15–25 Helles Avenue
Moorebank
NSW 2170
AUSTRALIA

Kiri Martin
Transworld Publishers (NZ) Ltd
3 William Pickering Drive
Albany
Auckland
NEW ZEALAND

SWEET VALLEY HIGH™

The top-selling teenage series starring identical twins Jessica and Elizabeth Wakefield and all their friends at Sweet Valley High. Don't miss the latest mini-series published as part of this successful series!